MY PREROGATIVE

SASHA WHITE

HEAT
NEW YORK, NEW YORK

THE BERKLEY PUBLISHING GROUP
Published by the Penguin Group
Penguin Group (USA) Inc.
375 Hudson Street, New York, New York 10014, USA
Penguin Group (Canada), 90 Eglinton Avenue East, Suite 700, Toronto, Ontario M4P 2Y3, Canada
(a division of Pearson Penguin Canada Inc.)
Penguin Books Ltd., 80 Strand, London WC2R 0RL, England
Penguin Group Ireland, 25 St. Stephen's Green, Dublin 2, Ireland (a division of Penguin Books Ltd.)
Penguin Group (Australia), 250 Camberwell Road, Camberwell, Victoria 3124, Australia
(a division of Pearson Australia Group Pty. Ltd.)
Penguin Books India Pvt. Ltd., 11 Community Centre, Panchsheel Park, New Delhi—110 017, India
Penguin Group (NZ), 67 Apollo Drive, Rosedale, North Shore 0632, New Zealand
(a division of Pearson New Zealand Ltd.)
Penguin Books (South Africa) (Pty.) Ltd., 24 Sturdee Avenue, Rosebank, Johannesburg 2196,
South Africa

Penguin Books Ltd., Registered Offices: 80 Strand, London WC2R 0RL, England

This is an original publication of The Berkley Publishing Group.

This is a work of fiction. Names, characters, places, and incidents either are the product of the author's imagination or are used fictitiously, and any resemblance to actual persons, living or dead, business establishments, events, or locales is entirely coincidental. The publisher does not have any control over and does not assume any responsibility for author or third-party websites or their content.

MY PREROGATIVE

First edition: September 2008

Library of Congress Cataloging-in-Publication Data

White, Sasha, 1969-
    My prerogative / Sasha White. — 1st ed.
        p.   cm.
    ISBN 978-0-425-22340-6 (trade pbk.)
    I. Title.
    PS3623.H57885M9   2008
    813'.6—dc22   2008018332

PRINTED IN THE UNITED STATES OF AMERICA

10   9   8   7   6   5   4   3   2   1

Acknowledgments

Working nights can be different. Working in a nightclub is a whole 'nother world. As a bartender myself, I know this firsthand. Kelsey's story will hopefully give just a glimpse of that world to you.

Many thanks go out to Stewart Ingram for the help and advice on the Vancouver area. It's been too long since I've been in the city.

I'd also like to thank Cindy Hwang for letting me go with the story I wanted to write, and Roberta Brown for always being there.

I find sometimes it's easy to be myself.
Sometimes I find it's better to be somebody else.

—Dave Matthews Band

1

There are few things more enjoyable than lying naked on a sandy beach under a hot sun. Especially in a foreign country where no one knows me and I'm free to do whatever, and whomever, I want.

Kelsey Howard, footloose and fancy-free, answerable to no one. That was me.

Being single and adventurous made me the envy of many, and I had to admit, there were times when even *I* thought my life was blessed.

Cute as a kid, pretty as a girl, and then beautiful as a woman.

I do believe people see that when they look at me. I have to believe it; I've heard it my whole life. And on some days, I can even look in the mirror and see it. The problem is that I don't always feel that way. I have a hole inside that needs to be filled, and despite the fact that I know filling it with food, drinks, and casual sex isn't good, or smart . . . I still do it. I can't stop myself. It's the only way I know to fill that emptiness.

So, really? Is it wrong if it makes me feel better? Even if it's just for a little while?

Rising up a bit from my supine position on the beach, my elbows dug comfortably into the sand. I lounged in the heat of the Mediterranean sun and tracked the approach of my companion from behind dark sunglasses. *Nope, nothing wrong with it at all.*

Ocean water glistened over his bulging muscles as they rippled with every move he made. Hair slicked back and eyes intent on me, he prowled up the beach. Yeah, he was definitely prowling, and I was woman enough to appreciate it.

One of the few things I enjoy in life more than lying on a beach is lying under a well-built man. Both at once was a fantasy I was determined to finally have come true.

Marco was his name, and I'd met him at the hotel bar on my second night here. The all-inclusive resort we were at encouraged hedonistic behavior, and after the first night spent watching everyone let loose, I was more than ready for my own sensual adventure. I'd almost given up hope of finding someone I could click with when he'd introduced himself and the sparks flew. Marco had proven to be very adventurous—a wonderful choice for my holiday fling.

I took a pull of tequila from the bottle I'd grabbed from the room's minibar and a familiar tingle awoke low in my belly. Marco drew closer and I spread my legs a little wider, knowing he wouldn't be able to avoid the temptation I presented.

Sure enough, hunger sparked in his dark eyes and he dropped to his knees at my feet. Large masculine hands cupped my bent knees and slid up my thighs, sending more tingles through my system.

"Hello there, stranger," I said softly.

His teeth flashed in a predatory smile and he began crawling up and over my body until his mouth hovered over mine. "You look good enough to eat," he said.

I looked to the left and saw no one, and then to the right. There was a couple about fifty yards down the beach, roasting themselves on a blanket and minding their own business, so I lifted my arms and pulled him down on top of me. "So what's stopping you?"

He chuckled and kissed me hungrily. He tasted faintly of tequila and salt water from the ocean, so I opened up and enjoyed the way our tongues rubbed together. The cool friction heated my blood and made my sex clench in anticipation. The nude beach we were on was part of the private resort where anything goes, and in that instant I made the decision to live up to my reputation as a wild child and enjoy every second of it.

I tilted my head back, and Marco took the hint, nuzzling his way down my neck. The sound of waves rhythmically lapping at the shore became an erotic symphony as he cupped my breasts and flicked the jeweled hoops there back and forth.

"So pretty," he crooned. He wrapped his lips around one nipple and sucked hard, his tongue pulling at the piercing.

"Harder," I urged him. A little pain always heightened the pleasure.

He complied and my hips jerked in response. *Yes.*

I slid my hands into his hair and nudged him lower. Eager to please, Marco slithered down my body until his talented mouth was hovering over my greedy cunt. His hands cupped my ass, lifting me as his tongue came out and flicked the jeweled hoop that pierced the protective hood of my clit. A sigh of pleasure slipped from between my lips and I pressed him closer.

Sometimes fantasies do come true.

2

The flight home was smooth and easy. After I passed through customs and caught sight of the mob at baggage claim, I was doubly glad I'd packed light.

Heading through the automatic doors, I ignored the crowd of people eagerly waiting for arrivals to well . . . arrive. No one there was waiting for me.

It was late afternoon but the sun was shining down on Vancouver. The sky was clear and the air was so humid my hair began to wilt and immediately go flat. It didn't bother me though; I just reached into my purse for a couple of elastics and made two pigtails. Not many women my age could get away with the style, but I didn't look my age, and I certainly didn't feel it, so why care?

I knew the airport's parking lot layout well, so it took me no time to find my car. Dropping my bags on the passenger seat of the little red Camry, I climbed in, rolled down the window, and cranked up the tunes. I bopped along mindlessly to the music for the forty-five minute drive home, weaving in and out of the busy Saturday afternoon traffic but not letting the heat or the cranky drivers on the road get to me.

An hour after my feet touched the ground I was strolling into my apartment and dropping my bag on the floor while my stomach growled angrily. A quick peek into the fridge showed only a bottle of wine and a tub of margarine.

Why the hell hadn't I stopped at McDonald's or something on the way home? *Smart, Kelsey. Way to think ahead.*

There's nothing special about my apartment, other than the fact that it's all mine. I'd spent some time and money making it the best it could be, and that was a nice semistylish place with an eclectic collection of comfortable furniture, and all the amenities.

The thought of coming home to a messy place always had me on a cleaning spree the week before I went on any trip, and this last one had been no different. When I glanced around this time I noted that it looked as neat and clean as it had been when I left.

It was nice to come home to a clean place, but the hollowness of the empty apartment was a bit too much for me, so I dug out my iPod and put it in its cradle. Soon Dave Matthews was chasing the silence away and I reached for the phone.

I'd just finished ordering pizza for delivery and was opening the bottle of wine when there was a knock on the door. Yay! Someone came to welcome me home. *Not.*

Corkscrew still in hand, I opened it to one of the downstairs tenants.

"Hi, Manny, what can I do for you?"

A twenty-dollar bill was waved in front of my face. "My wife, she need the laundry tokens."

Manny was from Chile, and had lived on the first floor of the three-story building for the past twelve years. He and his wife were quiet and clean, and the first ones to welcome me to the complex when I'd moved in five years earlier, and I really liked them. Having neighbors who knew my name and were willing to water my plants while I was away made me feel a part of the place. "Sure. Wait right here."

I went to the kitchen and pulled the little plastic case from the cupboard. I was counting out tokens when Manny stepped into the open doorway. "Our kitchen sink is still dripping, Ms. Kelsey. It's very loud and keeps me awake at night. When will it get fixed?"

"I told you before. You have to phone Paul. He's the head of the condo board and in charge of things until the new building manager is here next month. I'm just taking care of the tokens and the basic maintenance for this month. I have nothing to do with repairs."

"Two weeks ago I call *el presidente*. He said he'd call a repairman, but I've not heard nothing, so I ask you again."

I shook my head and handed him the tokens with a soft smile. "I'm sorry, I haven't heard anything. I know it's annoying, but apparently the guy that the condo board hired is worth waiting for, and after the last manager, we need to make sure this new one knows what he's doing."

"That's true," he said, nodding his head thoughtfully. "That last guy did nothing but drink. He tried to fix the leak, and it only get worse."

"Less than a month to go, Manny." I ushered him out of the doorway. "I'll make sure when I meet the new building manager that your faucet is first on his to-do list."

I closed the door behind the grumbling old guy and went back to my bottle of wine. Sure I'd agreed to clean the building and hand out laundry tokens for the six weeks they were without a manager, but that was it. I was a bartender, not a handym—handy woman.

Two minutes later I was sitting down with wineglass in hand and the phone rang. I recognized Randy's number on the caller ID and decided I wasn't in the mood for a visit. Strange, normally a visit from my occasional and very adventurous lover was welcome, but right then, I just wanted to be alone with my wine.

Sunday was my day to get organized again before I returned to the regular programming of my uneventful life.

Still feeling pretty relaxed and genial after my holiday, I crawled out of bed around ten—which was actually early for me, the bartender who rarely went to bed before four in the morning. After a lazy shower I dressed in a casual pair of black walking shorts and a tight tank top that hugged my breasts and showed plenty of my C-cup cleavage. Hair wasn't something I wanted to deal with so I slipped a ball cap over my plain midnight tresses and smoothed on some bright red lipstick to finish the look before heading to the grocery store.

Vancouver is a big city, which makes housing in the decent areas pretty expensive. Commercial Drive, my neighborhood, was ethnically diverse and a bit seedy, but the city was working on cleaning it up. Cafés and restaurants were popping up all over and it had turned into a more eclectic, almost artsy area because of the recently restored lofts and buildings.

Grabbing a basket just inside the door, I filled it with pre-washed and cut bag salad, baby carrots, and celery before adding some peaches and heading for the frozen food aisle. Microwave dinners, pizza, and a carton of ice cream joined the healthy stuff. A basket full of essentials for a single person.

Staring at the food I'd collected was slightly depressing and I fought the temptation of the cookie aisle. Temptation won and I added a bag of chocolate chip to my basket. Not a coffee drinker, a pack of Red Bull energy drinks was the final item on my list.

The cashier smiled at me when I started to unload my items onto the conveyor belt and I smiled back. "Hi, Kelsey, how are you doing today?" she said when the customer ahead of me was done and walking away.

"Doing good, Maureen. You?"

Living alone made it hard to keep lots of food in my fridge because if I didn't eat at home every day, the food went bad. Which meant I didn't buy a lot, but I went food shopping two or three times a week. Since I'd been living in the same apartment for almost five years, and the grocery store was only four blocks away, a couple of the cashiers knew me by name.

I was a regular.

A chuckle bubbled up and Maureen grinned and shook her head in puzzlement. "You're always in such a good mood."

I wasn't really in a good mood, I was just amused because after bartending for fifteen years I'd always sworn I'd never be a "regular" anywhere. Regulars could keep a business going, but by the same token, they could be a real pain in the ass at times. But Maureen didn't need to hear all that so I just shrugged. "The sun is shining and I have nothing to complain about."

"Ahh." The pretty cashier nodded. "Well, here's hoping the rest of the week remains the same for us both."

She took my money, we said good day to each other, and I left with a smile still on my face. I had a date with a pitcher of margaritas I didn't want to be late for.

3

My timing was perfect.

I made my way through the crowded tables of Vantage Sports Pub to the patio where my friend waited. I made it to the plastic deck chair waiting for me mere seconds before the waitress arrived with a pitcher of frozen margaritas.

"How was Jamaica?" Dee McDonald asked as my butt hit the chair.

I thought of Marco and the secluded beach escapade. "In a word . . . delicious."

Dee was the manager of an Irish pub near the university and my best friend for the past fifteen years, ever since we met in college. Only two years apart in age, and both working in the hospitality industry, we understood each other in ways that only close friends and other waitresses could. But even Dee only understood that part of me. She didn't get that I was always searching for—well, searching.

Hell, even I didn't really know for sure what it was I was searching for. I just knew there had to be more to life than what was in front of me, and I wasn't going to find out what it was by living by someone else's rules.

"Only a masochist would go to the Caribbean in August," Dee said, distracting me from my thoughts.

The server set frosty glasses on the table and Dee poured us each a margarita from the pitcher while I answered.

"It was cheap, and not much hotter than this. Plus, the occasional afternoon thunderstorm cooled things off nicely." I eyed her. Dee's brunette hair was streaked blond and cut in a short bob. "And how were things in McDonald-land while I was gone? I like the new haircut, by the way. Very playful and summery."

"Thanks! Last week work sucked, and Jason fell asleep on the sofa every night, but the weekend was great. We got the backyard landscaped and the basement is almost finished. Oh, and Jason picked up a bunch of fitness equipment, including a cross trainer, so instead of meeting at the gym we can work out in the basement if we want."

I ignored the twinge of longing at the mention of comfortable married life and focused on the second half of what Dee said.

Jason was Dee's husband, and gorgeous as that man was, I didn't want to be working out in *any* basement.

"Sweetie, you're forgetting that one of the reasons I work

out at the gym is so I can drool over all the hot male hard-bodies that hang out there. What fun would working out in your basement be?"

"Jason will be there, and I know you think he's hot. He thinks you're pretty too, so you two can just drool over each other."

I rolled my eyes. "Get real. Jason can't see anyone else when you're around. Not that he'd drool over me anyway."

It was Dee's turn to roll her eyes. "You get real, you're like a cross between a fifties pinup model and the modern Goth Girl. If Marilyn Monroe was a thirtysomething right now, she'd look like you. Well, with black hair. The point is, all you have to do is smile and bat your eyelashes and men drool over you."

"Yeah?" I couldn't help myself, Dee had hit a sensitive spot. "First off, I'm not a goth, I just happen to have a unique sense of style. And second, is that why I'm almost thirty-five and still single? Because I'm so pretty that all I have to do is smile and men drool?"

"No," she said and waved her hand dismissively. "You're still single because you *want* to be single. Anytime a guy tries to get closer to you than your bed, you sabotage the relationship."

That was because when men found out how much I enjoyed sex, that was all they saw. They stopped seeing me as anything more than a real-life blow-up doll, and I wanted more than that. I deserved more than that.

"If I wanted to be single, I wouldn't have put that stupid personal ad online," I muttered.

"How's that going, anyway?"

"It's not." I watched over Dee's shoulder as the couple at the table behind her leaned together and kissed. It was a slow, seductive kiss, with the guy cupping the woman's cheek in his hand as he looked into her eyes. It was the kind of kiss I dreamt about.

"Kelsey?"

"Huh?" I tore my gaze away from the couple and focused on the conversation. Where were we? Oh yeah, the online thing. I drained the last of my margarita and made light of it all. "After chatting online to more guys than I thought possible, I gave it up as hopeless about a month ago."

"Hopeless? Really?"

Well, except for Randy. But Randy wasn't a boyfriend, he was occasional . . . exercise. He filled a need, that was it. But I didn't say that. Dee might be my closest friend, but there were some things even I preferred to keep private.

"Yeah, only a few of the men were interesting enough to actually meet for a drink. And of course, the ones I'm attracted to aren't interested in me, and vice versa. It's easier to just stick with what I have." Which is a lover who was happy to come when I called, share a drink or two, fuck, then leave.

"What about the gym?" Dee asked.

"No one ever hits on me at the gym." I caught the waitress's eye and she nodded. Another pitcher was on the way.

"Maybe if you didn't wear headphones someone would try to chat you up."

"I tried that actually. And you know what I noticed?"

"What?"

"That everyone else was wearing headphones."

Dee shook her head and I laughed.

"What about the grocery store?" Dee said determinedly. "You love to cook and I know you hit the market at least twice a week."

I waved my hand. "Urban myth."

"Ha! You're just too damn picky."

That got me.

"I'm not too picky," I snapped. "I just know myself, and what I need to be happy. So you're right, I am single because I want to be."

"What do you need, then?"

Tequila had loosened my tongue enough that I didn't even think about it. "I want someone who will see below the surface and be *in love* with me. I want someone who wants more than to see me happy. I want someone who wants to *make me* happy.

"I want someone that makes *me* want to please *him*. I know it's almost archaic but I want someone to cook for. Someone to sit on the couch and veg with as well as someone I can give a look to, who'll be able to read it. He'll know when I want to kill him, and when I want to ravish him. Or when I want him to slam me against the wall and have his way with me." *And I want him to accept that sometimes, he alone won't be enough for me.*

Dee's brows puckered. "There's nothing wrong with wanting the fantasy, Kels. But you have to understand that not everyone gets it."

"Did it ever occur to you that not everyone gets it because not everyone is willing to wait for it?"

Dee stared at me blankly. I'd shocked her. Shit, I'd shocked myself. My façade was cracking and real emotions were starting to leak out. I had to stop that. Now.

All I'd ever really admitted to myself was that I'd rather be on my own than waste my time in a relationship that wasn't everything I wanted. Everything I needed. Self-analysis was good, sometimes it even helped, but I did not need anyone thinking I was some lonely chick who needed a man to make her life complete. I worked damn hard to convince everyone who knew me that I was completely happy with every aspect of my single life.

I worked even harder to convince myself.

The shock in Dee's eyes had faded and I could clearly see concern building. *Shit.*

Relief swept over me when the waitress set a fresh jug of margaritas down. Dee grimaced. I poured myself another.

"I work in a nightclub, Dee. I see people fucking around and cheating on their partners all the time. That's what happens when people settle, and I'm not going to do that. I have to believe there's someone out there for me. Someone who will love the hyperactive, outgoing, and flirty me, as much as the somewhat dark and twisted me. If there isn't, then I don't want anyone." I grinned at my friend. "Not on a permanent basis, anyway."

Dee laughed and shook her head. "That's probably best. It'll happen when you least expect it, it always does. Besides, you're too busy traveling all over and playing sex games with your bed buddies to settle down right now. If you weren't single you wouldn't be able to do that. You certainly wouldn't have been able to pick up some stranger and fuck him on the beach in Jamaica." She winked at me. "Lucky bitch. How was it?"

I choked on a mouthful of margarita. "How do you know I even did that?"

"You said you were going to, and you *always* do what you say you're going to. Now stop stalling and tell me how it was. I'm a boring old married woman. I need to live vicariously through you."

"Boring maybe, but not old," I stated firmly. "I'm older than you and I'm not old. So that means you're not old yet, either."

Dee raised her glass and tilted her head. "Point taken."

The waitress came by to check on us and I ordered a couple of tequila shots.

"One shot, and that's it," Dee warned. "The last time we got into the shooters, Jason wouldn't talk to me for the rest of the weekend. Funny how he gets mad at me when I have a few drinks, yet every time he comes home from playing golf, he's hammered."

I bit my tongue and took another sip of frosty lime loveliness. Dee had no idea how much I envied her relationship with Jason, and I wanted to keep it that way. There were times when booty calls and bed buddies were fun and exciting, but there were also times when coming home to an empty apartment sucked.

The waitress dropped off the tequila shots and I was quick to reach for mine. "To a man who loves you," I said and raised my glass in a toast.

Dee raised her glass and clinked it against mine. "To living out the fantasy of fucking a stranger on a beach."

For the next couple of hours Dee and I talked about work, clothes, Jamaica, Marco, and our hopes for the upcoming hockey season. The pub crowd thinned as time passed and people moved on to whatever plans they had for the evening. Just after four o'clock, Dee announced it was time to go.

"You go," I replied. "I'm going to stay awhile longer."

She dug some cash out of her wallet and put it on the table beneath her empty glass. "Must be nice. I get to go home and cook dinner for a man who'll probably just fall asleep on the couch the minute he's done eating."

"So wake him up," I said, tired of her whining.

"Easier said than done, my friend."

One of my biggest pet peeves is when people complain about something, yet do nothing to change it. Like a wife complaining about her husband falling asleep on the sofa. As far as I was concerned, where there's a will, there's a way. And the easiest way was sometimes the best.

"Use sex. He's a man, that'll wake him up."

"Use sex? Hell, I'd be thrilled to have sex tonight. It's been almost a week, and last time it was barely over before he started snoring."

"That's sad."

"Tell me about it." She slumped back in her seat. "We had

sex more often before we were married. You're single and you have more sex than we do."

That really is sad.

If I were married, you'd bet the man would be giving it to me every night. Otherwise divorce would be inevitable—unless he didn't mind me having sex with others. I could probably live with that.

I gave my head a shake. It was time to focus on Dee. "So liven it up," I told her. "Wake him up in a way he'll never forget, and maybe he'll be a little more energetic for the rest of the night."

Dee's eyes lit up and she leaned forward, her purse still clutched in her lap. "Tell me, Oh Wise Wild One, how should I do that?"

Excitement rippled through me.

I loved sex. I thought about sex all the time. Positions, scenarios, certain people, combinations of people, different ways to masturbate, different kinks. Over the years I'd found that there were few problems or issues that either alcohol or sex couldn't cure.

Temporarily anyway . . . I was still working on the long-term cure.

Mind you, falling asleep on the sofa sounded short-term to me. "Do you guys ever role-play?"

Her brows puckered. "Role-play? As in the Naughty Nurse and her bedridden patient?"

I laughed. "Yeah, that's one type of role-playing. You guys ever do anything like that?"

"We tried it once, but I couldn't stop laughing."

Dee and I have been friends for a long time, and while she wasn't as . . . open as I was, I remembered our drunk partying nights pretty clearly. She wasn't as angelic as her big brown eyes led people to believe either.

"After dinner, tell him you're going to the bedroom, and be sure to give him *the look*."

"The look?"

"Yeah. The one that says 'Follow me, I'm horny.' "

"Oh, *that* look." Dee laughed. "Okay. Got it."

"When you're upstairs, find some sexy lingerie—matching bra and panties, garter and thigh highs, baby doll nightgown—whatever you have that you know gets him hard and will make him drool."

A secretive smile spread across Dee's lips and I knew she instantly had an outfit in mind.

"If he hasn't followed you into the bedroom by the time you've changed and are ready, then go get out the vacuum."

"The vacuum?"

"If he's asleep on the sofa, it'll wake him up. If he's not, he'll still notice you. Just go about the cleaning, as if you had on sweatpants and a T-shirt. Bending here, stretching there." I gave her a stern look. "But ignore him."

Dee's eyes were round and she was grinning like an idiot. "Oh my God," she said. "That will drive him absolutely nuts."

"There you go." I nodded. "The rest is up to you, but I suggest if you have to take out the vacuum, you make him work for it."

We shared another chuckle and Dee jumped up. "Okay, I'm outta here. I'll call you."

"I'm gonna want details."

4

I sat in the cheap plastic chair at the little patio table all by myself and people-watched for a while. I'd had a bit to drink, and I needed to kill some time before I drove home.

My mind kept going back to the online dating thing. Dee had been harping on me for years to stop being so open about my sexuality. That no matter what men said, the old double standard was still there. Good girls didn't have sex on the first date, and bad girls were only good for sex.

I told her I refused to believe it . . . but in reality, I believed it. I just refused to let it change who I was or how I acted. And I'd paid for it.

The online thing had been intriguing for a month or so, but it ended up being nothing but demoralizing. All that talking and flirting through e-mails only to meet the guys and find out either (A) there was absolutely no chemistry at all or (B) they were liars.

There had been one or two that I'd had great chemistry with, and great sex too, but that had been it. The worst thing about the online dating fiasco had been that it had gotten my hopes up. It had seemed a great way to meet guys outside the bar, but in all reality, the men online were worse than the ones in the bar. At least the guys in the bar didn't try to pretend they wanted more than what they did, which was usually a night or two of hot sex, with no promises.

The guys online handed out a bunch of crap about looking for a relationship and love. The majority of the time I'd meet with them, and silly me, think we were forming a connection, only to discover that once they got laid, I never heard from them again. I was all for a night of hot, dirty sex with a stranger, no strings attached, but I didn't like being lied to.

Whatever. I might be willing to give up the hunt for love, but I was *not* going to give up sex. It was one of the few things that kept me sane.

All that thinking about sex had erotic heat thrumming through my veins and a dampness forming between my thighs. Dee knew I had more than one lover, but she had no idea just how addicted to it all I'd become over the years. One glance around the pub showed me there were no single men to hit on and my frustration rose.

Then I got mad at myself. "Jesus, Kelsey, you just got laid for a week straight. Give yourself a time-out," I muttered to myself.

To make sure I didn't follow the urge to troll through my phone index for a man to fuck, I flipped open my cell and dialed from memory. "Hey little sis, what are you up to tonight?"

"Kelsey! I thought you were on a beach somewhere?"

"That was last week. Keep up, would ya?"

Ariel's light laugh echoed over the phone line. "Sorry. It's tough having a jet-setting sister, y'know. What's up?"

"I haven't seen you in a while and I thought I'd invite you over to dinner tonight. I have a new recipe I want to try out." I didn't have a new recipe, but cooking and eating were second only to sex on my list of life's simple pleasures. And beaches. Yeah, lying on beaches was up there on that list too.

"Ohhhh." Ariel moaned into the phone. "It sounds so good. You know I love your cooking, but I have to finish addressing these freak'n wedding invitations."

"Do that tomorrow."

"I can't. It's the fifteenth and I have to get them done or Miles's mother will never let me live it down."

I snorted. "Procrastinated as long as you could, huh?" Ariel was the queen of the last-minute detail. Speaking of which. "Have you found a dress yet?"

"I don't want to talk about that," she said crisply. Then her voice took on a hopeful tone. "Since you don't have a date tonight, you could come over and help me with the invitations."

"Um, no." I laughed. "I think I'll stay away from the homestead while it's all caught up in wedding fever. It's not my style. But you be sure to call me whenever you need to get away from it all."

Ariel promised and we hung up.

Restless energy had me up and out of my seat in seconds. I

tossed some cash on the table to match Dee's and headed out of the pub.

The closer I got to home, the hornier I became. By the time I parked my car and strode up the stairs to my apartment I had a clear plan, if not a clear head. I pulled my toy chest out from under my bed, stripped off my clothes, and went back to the living room with my hands full.

Since it was the middle of August, my place was still flooded with sunlight, even though it was just dinnertime. I'd kept the curtains closed in the vain hope that my unit wouldn't turn into an oven. Despite my lack of clothing, a layer of sweat popped up on my skin within seconds.

Uncaring of my nakedness, I pushed back the heavy curtains that shaded the room and slid the patio door open.

It was sort of weird to be standing on my own deck in the nude in broad daylight, but freeing too. I loved the sun on my naked skin when I was on a foreign beach, but I'd always tried to keep that part of my life separate. When I was home, I worked, I hung out with friends, and I . . . worked some more.

When I was away from home, I truly played.

Only I needed to play now.

The DVD player was in the corner of the room right next to the patio doors and I loaded the disk into it before going to take a chair from the kitchen. I set the chair a couple feet in front of the TV, with the back to the screen.

The movie loaded and I flipped through the menu to my favorite scene. Then, pulling the six-inch silicone cock out of its silk storage sack, I slapped it onto the chair and grinned when the suction cup on the bottom took hold.

The next best thing to the real deal.

Flopping on the sofa, I watched as the woman onscreen got on her knees between two naked men and started sucking one cock, then the other. I cupped my breasts and tugged on the nipples until they were red and tight, shooting pleasure straight to my core. When the moaning on-screen started to get loud, I remembered the open patio door and turned the volume down with one hand while the other traveled over my belly to my sex.

Thinking about sex for the last hour had me so excited my clit was already hard and sensitive. I tugged on the piercing, rubbed the jewel against my clit once, twice, three times and I was up. This was not going to take long at all.

Bracing my hands on the back, I swung my leg over the chair and let the head of the dildo nudge my entrance. Tilting my head, I inched lower, my thigh muscles starting to tremble with the strain of going slow. The head breached my entrance and I lowered myself onto the dildo.

I was wet and more than ready, but with no lube it was still a tight fit.

Pain mixed with the pleasure and I pushed down harder as I watched the girl on-screen get a cock shoved up her pussy from behind while the second guy fucked her mouth. They were a wickedly beautiful trio.

Finally it was all the way in and I was so full a guttural moan ripped from my throat. Fuck, I loved being full. I loved the tinge of pain that shaded the pleasure soaring through my system. I loved the raw naughtiness of fucking myself in broad daylight while the scandalous sounds of the porn filled the room.

With my feet planted on the floor and juices flowing so fast, I was soon bouncing up and down, and moaning louder than the people on-screen. Sweat slicked my body and my insides clenched. This time when I thought about the open curtains, the sunlight, and the fact that someone might hear me, my cunt clenched. I closed my eyes and imagined the hand that reached down between my legs wasn't mine. Rough fingers circled my clit, tugging on it until my back arched and my mouth opened in a silent scream of pleasure.

I sat for a minute, still full of fake cock, with my arms folded across the back of the chair and my head resting on top of them. The grunting, panting, and sighing coming from the TV told me I'd beaten my celluloid friends to the finish line, and I laughed.

5

She was glorious.

Harlan Shaw stood near the window of his loft and stared across the street in amazement. He wasn't in the habit of spying on his neighbors. He'd been staring out the window chasing his muse when a movement had caught his attention, and he'd focused on the naked woman opening her patio door.

A petite but well-rounded woman with curves and softness in all the right places. A woman with breasts that jiggled with every move and hips rounded enough to get a good grip on.

When she'd dropped onto the couch and started playing with those breasts, Harlan had been a bit surprised. He didn't know many women bold enough to run around naked in broad daylight, let alone masturbate.

He stepped closer to the window and watched, mesmerized as she played with herself. When she'd stood up and straddled the chair in the middle of the room, he finally noticed the rubber dick sticking up out of it and realized he'd found his missing muse.

"Such a dirty girl," he murmured in appreciation.

The sun danced over her skin as her breasts bounced, and she rode that cock. Harlan's own hand covered his crotch and his thumb stroked the hardness beneath his zipper. He could easily take himself out and join her in her naughtiness, but he didn't want to be distracted. He just wanted to watch.

The expression on her face, the way she moved, and the way her hips swiveled . . . she was pure animal in heat. There was no pretense or coyness, no tentativeness at all in her movements. She was on the hunt for pleasure, and it was intoxicating to watch.

Her head went back, black hair streaming over her arched back as her breasts thrust forward, the tips glinting in the sunlight. Harlan held his breath, his eyes glued to her face as her eyes closed and her lips parted.

Christ, how he wanted to hear her scream.

6

On Monday night the energy was high at Risqué nightclub and I was rockin' it out behind the bar. The heavy beat of the music had my blood pumping and my hips swinging as I poured drinks and collected money with an ease born of too many years on the job. The holiday was over, and I was back in the swing of real life.

"Next!" I called out as one customer turned away from the bar with a Paralyzer in each hand.

A good-looking, muscle-bound guy stepped up to the bar with a big grin. "Hey, baby. We missed you here last week," he said.

"Sorry, Jack." I flashed him my patented wicked grin. "I was too busy lying naked on a beach in Jamaica to come to work."

The bouncer from one of the downtown clubs hooted, his eyes roving over my chest appreciatively.

"I wish I'd been there. Maybe you'll show me your lack of tan lines later?" His eyebrows jumped suggestively and I laughed.

"It *was* a good time. What can I get you tonight?"

Just then a second hottie stepped up to the bar. "C'mon Jack. Drinks now, flirt later."

"Back off," Jack snapped at his friend and I bit back another laugh.

Jack smiled at me and ordered a couple of beers before turning and mumbling something to his buddy. The guy probably wasn't even twenty-five, but Jack had been flirting with me for months. Every time he came into the bar he asked me to go home with him at the end of the night. It was flattering, and I'd been tempted to take him up on it a time or two, but I'd learned my lesson years ago. Fucking the regulars was a bad idea.

Plus, I wondered if he knew that I was ten years older than him if he'd still give it a shot. Or maybe he did know, and that was my appeal. Maybe he wanted to be schooled by an older woman.

I gave a mental shrug. Stranger things had happened.

Setting the two beers on the bar, I quirked an eyebrow at the boys. "Any shots to get your juices flowing?"

That was all it took. Jack ordered three tequilas, straight up.

One of the keys to the bar making money is shooters. Sex on the Beach, Blow Jobs, Porn Stars, Tequila, Gladiators, Sambuca . . . and most customers didn't know until they walked up to the bar that they really wanted a shot. It was my job to lead the way by making sure they associated drinking shots with a damn good time.

I pulled the bottle out of the ice well and with a flip of the wrist spun it around my hand until it was upside down and filling the lined up shot glasses. I dropped it back into the well and smiled. "Twenty-seven even, Jack."

He handed me the money and nudged a tequila closer to me. "For you." He and his friend picked up the other two, we clinked glasses and shot them back. The slight burn down my throat was pleasant and my insides warmed.

"Thank you, gentlemen."

Jack's friend leaned on the bar and put his hand over mine. "Now that the drinks are out of the way, what's your name, sweetness?"

Oooh, this one thought he was a real stud.

Jack gestured to his friend. "Kelsey, this idiot is my buddy Dave, visiting for a week from back home. Dave, Kelsey's the shit. Don't mess with her."

With a wink at Jack, I leaned forward and smiled pretty for Dave. "And I'm definitely not sweet, little boy."

"I'd be happy to prove that I'm anything but little," he tossed back with a chuckle and a leer worthy of a true pervert.

There was a clear light of intrigue in his eyes. The guy was good-looking, but it was obvious he wasn't used to having to work for his women. Which just made me want to work him up some more before I turned him down.

Yeah, I could be a real tease when I wanted.

"Size doesn't matter if you don't know what to do with it."

"Let me show you what I can do with it."

"Dude, Kelsey don't do pretty boys like you," Jack said. "Leave her alone so she can do her job."

I winked at Jack and blew him a kiss as he pulled his friend away from the bar. Dave would be back to take another run at me; some guys could never resist a challenge, especially the young, cocky ones.

With nothing to do for a minute, I just stood there and absorbed the energy of the club.

Like any nightclub, Risqué was dark inside, but that's where the similarities ended. The converted warehouse was huge, with an upstairs VIP area and a couple of pool tables, and a separate room under the stairs for private bookings. The dance floor was in the middle of the place with a raised stage at the front, four cages surrounding it, and colored lights flickering over it all to the beat of the music.

Valentine Ward, the owner of the club and my boss, hired dancers, both male and female, to occupy the cages. While the dancers wore club gear, often showing plenty of skin, they weren't strippers and the club maintained a very classy, yet decadent and uninhibited, atmosphere. It catered to a clientele that ranged from young and cocky, like Jack and Dave, to businessmen, and hockey stars of the NHL.

Most bars were quiet on Monday nights, with some of them not even bothering to open. Because of that, Val had dubbed Monday nights "Industry Night," and we always had a pretty good crowd.

Even better for me was that the crowd was small enough that I could work the front bar by myself (with one more bartender at the back bar and one upstairs in the VIP section, which we kept open to everyone on Mondays). But between the waitresses' runs and the bar service, there was enough drinking going on to keep me busy. And the fact that they were all waitresses, bartenders, bouncers, or other employees of clubs and pubs around the city made them good tippers.

On average, I made more on Monday nights than any other night, and I had a good time working it too.

"Can I call?"

I turned away from the dance floor and glanced at Callie, the only waitress on shift. So far. "What can I get ya?"

She called out her order, and I started putting it together.

"So?" Callie practically bounced in her excitement.

"So, what?"

"Did Jack finally ask you out?"

Callie was a pretty girl in her early twenties. Long black hair, porcelain skin, and naturally red lips. She showed some skin when she was at work, but being a farm girl from a small town, she didn't yet have the sexy or naughty aura that a lot of cocktail waitresses did, nor the cynicism.

I smiled at her innocence. "No, he didn't. And I doubt he ever will."

"Really?" A pucker formed between her delicately arched eyebrows. "But he likes you. I know he does. He never takes his eyes off you when he's here."

"That doesn't mean he likes *me*, sweetie. It means he likes the way I look." I saw her open her mouth to protest and I cut her off by holding up a hand. "And while he's never asked me out, he asks me to go home with him every time he comes in here."

Color flooded Callie's cheeks and I could see her getting insulted on my behalf. "It's okay, Callie. If he wasn't a regular here, I might actually take him up on it."

"Really?"

I bit back a chuckle as I put the last drink on her tray. She was so sweet. "Yes, really. I don't need to be in love to enjoy sex. But sex with regular customers is just asking for problems."

She eyed me shrewdly, ignoring the full tray of drinks in front of her. "Have you ever been in love, Kelsey?"

Caught off guard, I shook my head automatically. When Callie just nodded as if to say "I thought as much" and picked up her tray, I decided that maybe she wasn't as innocent as I'd thought.

An hour later I was serving a small group of girls upside-down margaritas and telling them dirty jokes when I saw Val wander by. After their second round of shots, the girls ordered some cocktails, giggling and posturing for my boss.

"You're such a brat, Kelsey," Val said from where he stood at the end of the bar after they left. "Teaching those innocent young things jokes like that."

Valentine Ward was a man you didn't want to fuck with, and if you had half a brain, you knew it just by looking at him. Built lean and lethal, he had long dark hair that he kept tied at the base of his skull, dark eyes, and an aura that could only be called intimidating. He always wore suits at the club, but the fancy clothes did nothing to hide his raw masculinity, or his strength.

"Me?" I pulled an innocent face at his comment. "Those girls were anything but innocent. If you doubt it, just crook your finger at one of them and see how fast her panties hit the floor."

He rolled his eyes and didn't look twice at the girls still drooling over him. I laughed and continued shaking my ass to the music.

Not many people got close enough to Val to see the wicked sense of humor he had, but I'd worked for him since he'd opened Risqué years ago, and we had a good relationship.

"You heading out?" I asked when I saw him jingling his keys in his hand.

"If you're good for the night."

I had all the knowledge and skills to be the manager at Risqué, but Val kept my title as head bartender because I'd asked him to. Helping him out by opening or closing the bar once or twice a week or doing the liquor orders occasionally was fine, but I didn't want the responsibilities on a regular basis. I enjoyed working behind the bar too much to give it up full-time.

"No worries here, boss. John is in the VIP and Steve is at the door, so I can close up. You go home and give Samair a treat." I wiggled my eyebrows and he chuckled.

"Like I said . . . brat."

"Go!"

Samair was Val's live-in girlfriend and I really liked her. She used to run her own lingerie design business out of the extra storage room upstairs, but recently moved to a small storefront, and I knew the couple wasn't getting as much time together as they'd like. Especially since I'd been gone for the past week, which meant Val had opened and closed every day.

Val slipped away from the bar and through the swinging door that led to the back alley entrance just as a song ended. Another line of customers began to form in front of me and I pasted a smile on my face.

7

The obnoxious ring of the phone woke me up the next morning and I answered it without opening my eyes. "Hello?"

"Are you still in bed, Kelsey?"

My mom.

"Yeah," I said as I rolled over in bed with the phone to my ear.

"It's almost noon."

I swallowed a sigh at the disapproval in her voice, and glanced at the clock. It wasn't even quarter past eleven. "Yeah, and I only went to bed at six."

My mother's sigh was not hidden. "You're not a young girl anymore, Kelsey. When are you going to grow up and put your education to use?"

"What do you want, Mom?"

"I'm calling about dinner on Sunday. I'm stuffing a turkey,

Ariel and Miles are coming over, and I was hoping you'd join us for dinner as well."

I tried to think fast but my brain was still asleep. "I have plans." It was lame, but it was all I could come up with.

"A date?"

"Just plans, Mom."

"Well, you know you could bring a date to dinner. It would be nice to meet your boyfriend."

I was waking up, and that wasn't necessarily a good thing. I was not a morning person. "Which one would you like to meet? I have a few, y'know."

"Isn't there anyone special?" Exasperation was clear in her voice. A mother could always hope.

"Nope," I said. "Besides, it's a moot point. I have plans so I can't make it to dinner." My only plan was to avoid as many family get-togethers as possible because I really didn't need to be reminded constantly that I wasn't living up to my parents' expectations.

Shit. I was thirty-four years old, you'd think I'd stop craving my mother's approval. But it was hard. Deep down I knew that the elusive thing I was always searching for was a place where I belonged. My family loved me, there was never any doubt in my mind about that, but I never quite fit in with them.

They were all very conservative, and quiet, and *normal*—and I wasn't. I liked my crazy job, body piercings, and funky fashions. Having a safe, secure job or getting married and having kids had never appealed to me. I accepted that being part of the neighborhood book club was enough excitement for Mom. I understood that all Ariel had ever wanted was to get married and start a family by the time she was thirty. I understood my dad just wanted a secure job and a steady paycheck. And yet none of them could understand why I didn't want any of those things.

"They need an intern and Marley said if you could drop off a resume today she'll get you an interview."

My mind had drifted as Mom talked about some job opening she'd heard about, but the word *interview* had caught my attention. "I'm not interested, Mom. A desk job would kill me slowly."

"Well you need to find something productive, Kelsey. This sleeping in until noon isn't healthy. Are you sure you're not depressed?"

"Mom, I *work* until three in the morning. It's not like I'm unemployed or something."

"Bartending isn't a real job, dear—"

"My other line is ringing, Mom. I have to go. I'll talk to you later, okay?"

I hung up before she could stop me. Then, for good measure, I turned the ringer off before I rolled over and went back to sleep. Another hour and I'd be human.

As soon as the apartment door swung closed behind me, my hands were on the buttons of my blouse. Then my pants hit the floor. Wearing nothing but my padded bra and panties, I grabbed a six-pack of beer from the fridge and headed for the balcony. Temperatures had been hitting record highs all week long and it was getting on my nerves. Thank God my second-floor apartment faced east so it was at least shaded by early evening. The air was still hot and humid, but the slight breeze that blew every now and then was a heavenly touch on my overheated skin.

After going to the gym, I'd spent the evening catching an early show in an air-conditioned movie theater. I loved movies, and I usually enjoyed going to them by myself. My popcorn was mine alone, and no one whispered in my ear, ruining things. But Friday night wasn't the best time to indulge in that pastime. All I'd done was make myself hyperaware of the couples and groups of people around me.

I stretched out on the lounger and gazed up at the sky as it darkened and the stars started to come out. It was Friday night and I was sitting on my balcony, all alone, drinking.

How sad was that?

After finishing my second beer, I debated going inside, but I was too comfortable where I was. Besides, why go inside when I'd just be alone in there too? At least outside I could hear traffic and the occasional voices carrying on the breeze. I could imagine there was someone out there who cared where I was—what I was doing.

I sighed, not bothering to wipe at the tears that were slowly leaking out. Lifting my face to the night breeze, I breathed deep. Coming home alone after the movie had been my own choice. I could've gone out.

I'd given Randy a call earlier, but he was out of town and

unable to help me out with a few hours of entertainment. I could've headed out to a pub or bar on my own, shot some pool, had a few drinks, found a man for the night, but that required a bit more energy than I had. I was tired. Tired of people telling me how lucky I was to be free and single. Tired of always looking for something I couldn't seem to find. So tired of the superficial greatness of my life.

I opened my eyes and searched the stars as another tear trickled out. I was being an idiot. PMS or some shit had drained all of my energy until I was beyond apathetic about everything in my life.

It was stupid too. I had a good life, really; how could it be otherwise when I had almost everything I'd ever wanted? In high school when all my friends were dreaming of getting married and popping out babies by the time they were twenty, I dreamt of seeing the world and having grand adventures. All I'd ever really wanted was to experience life—to really *live* it. And I had.

Only I'd experienced everything on my life's to-do list by the time I hit thirty, and now I was lost.

I could tell myself it didn't matter, but that would be lying.

"C'mon Kelsey, smarten up," I muttered. "Dee was right; if you really wanted a boyfriend, you could have one."

A boyfriend.

If only it were as simple as that.

Men had always been easy for me to get . . . but hard to keep. It had never bothered me before because I always figured that if it were meant to be, it would happen. If it was meant to be, when I pulled back, they wouldn't walk away without looking back.

Like that guy in Dublin a couple of years earlier, Jesse.

We'd had an instant connection. I'd felt it and he had too. "Do I know you?" he'd asked when we'd met in the street. "You look familiar."

He hadn't looked familiar, but he'd certainly made my heart go pitter-patter in my chest. It wasn't his looks either. He was cute, but nothing special. It had just been . . . a connection.

We'd spent all night together, talking and cuddling on the sofa in his hotel room. It had been the first time since I was a teenager that I'd spent all night in a man's arms and not had sex. And it had been intense. More intense than any time I'd ever spent with a guy before. At one point in the night, I'd looked at him and my breath had caught in my throat. The corners of his mouth had lifted and I'd spoken straight from the heart. "I could really fall in love with you," I'd said.

"I think I *have* fallen for you," he replied.

The silence between us at that had been comfortable. We'd connected.

Jesse was an American who was waiting in Dublin for a friend who was due in a couple of days, and then they were going to travel around the country. When I told him it was my last night in Dublin, he'd suggested spending the next few days traveling with me, up to Scotland. The idea had filled me with warmth, and I'd fallen asleep with an idiotic grin on my face.

But when morning arrived I'd untangled myself from his arms, smiled at him, and left without a word. And he'd let me. I went back to my own hotel room, packed my bags and left for the ferry station without contacting him again. By the time I'd arrived in Glasgow, I'd gotten over my fear and called the hotel where he'd been. I was hoping to maybe get his e-mail or some way to keep in touch, but he'd already checked out.

Maybe he'd been *the one* for me, and I'd let him go.

Then there was my friend Janelle's brother-in-law. He was before Jesse, when I was about twenty-six. Even though Dan was in his early thirties, he'd been sexy and I'd been tempted. If he'd asked to take me home, I would've gone with him eagerly. At that point in time most of my sexual experiences happened when I was too drunk for good old Catholic guilt to interfere with my body's needs. An older, more experienced man would've been an adventure worthy of more than a drunken night.

Only when Janelle had said Dan was in love with me, I'd immediately made the decision to never go to another of her family functions. Funny thing was, for a guy who'd said he was in love with me, he'd never once called and asked me out.

Ah, hell, it didn't matter now.

Convincing myself that all that was missing from my life was a man was a cop-out. I'd never been one of those women who wasn't happy unless she had a man in her life. I loved my job, I loved my little condo, and I have good friends. But I wanted more.

The real problem was, I didn't really know what the hell that more was.

One last look up at the stars in the night sky had some part of me still hoping for a storybook happily-ever-after. Maybe a falling star to make a wish on. Before I could spot one, a tingle skipped through me and I dragged my gaze from the stars above. It almost felt like . . . someone was watching me.

My gaze skimmed over the sidewalk beneath me, and up the side of the building across the street. Nothing. There were people around, but no one was paying attention to me. Whatever. I was just imagining things.

Straightening up, I spun on my heel and went back inside, careful to pull the drapes closed behind me.

8

Harlan set down his camera and stepped back from the window.
She was so beautiful it almost hurt to look at her. Sure she'd been wild and sexy and raw the afternoon he'd watched her masturbate, and since then he'd been unable to stop thinking about her. But moments ago, when she'd been on her balcony, staring at the stars, she'd looked like an angel with a bruised soul.

It called to him, that bruised part of her. So much more than her beauty.

He watched her from his loft, knowing that it was an intrusion, but unable to stop. He'd seen her in the afternoon, dancing around her apartment with her iPod on, and her obvious joy and verve had made him smile. Now, only hours later, she seemed so adrift.

For some reason it bothered him to think of her like that. He wanted to go to her, convince her she was beautiful and strong and vital. He wanted to wrap his arms around her and make her forget all her troubles.

Harlan rubbed his eyes and dragged his hands down his face when he saw the lights go out in her apartment.

He had to stop watching. He was becoming obsessed with a woman who didn't even know who he was. Talk about a fucked-up relationship.

9

I walked into the bar on Saturday night already in a weird mood. I'd tried to shake the emotional hangover from my pity party the night before, but it wasn't going so well, and I was getting grumpier by the minute. There was no room for *what if*s and *wish I had*s in life. Nothing good ever came from overanalyzing things you couldn't change, so why bother?

In an effort to get out of my own head before I went freakin' nuts, I cranked up the sound system and loaded in my CD of personal theme songs. Yep, I'd watched *Ally McBeal*, identifying with the neurotic lawyer in ways I never thought possible.

Bif Naked's "I Love Myself Today" filled the club and I made my way back to the bar. I was back there slicing fruit for the drinks when Val came down from his office upstairs, pulled up a stool and sat across from me.

"Hey, boss. Want a drink?"

"Beer," he said.

There was no need for me to ask what kind so I snagged his regular, popped the top, and set it in front of him before picking up the knife again.

It wasn't unusual for Val to sit and have a drink while I did the prep, but this time his stare was getting to me.

"What?" I finally snapped.

He took a swallow of beer then pinned me with his gaze. "You tell me."

"Nothing to tell." I shrugged and concentrated fiercely on the lime in front of me.

He waited me out. One night after I'd first started working for Val, I'd gotten too drunk when working the bar, and he'd called me on it. I was down and lonely, and feeling sorry for myself. My parents were pissed at me for letting my college degree sit unused while I tended bar. A guy I'd spent the night with had called me a freak, in the light of the morning after, of course. But my being a freak hadn't stopped him from enjoying my body the night before. Being drunk at the time that Val had called me out, I'd vomited out some shit about nobody else caring, so why should he?

It had been the wrong thing to say to a man who grew up with no family.

I'd finally confessed to him about how there were times when I felt so lost and alone I thought I'd go insane. How I knew it was stupid when I had a really great life, yet I couldn't seem to stop myself from drinking, fighting, and fucking. Those things calmed a part of me that I didn't understand. There was no tragedy in my background. No abuse, no deaths or illness. There was no real reason for the darkness that crouched within my soul.

For the first time in my life, someone had looked at me and not called me a freak, or crazy, or tried to make light of what I'd said by telling me how great my life was . . . how blessed I was.

Instead, Val had listened and convinced me that if doing those things calmed me, that was okay. He'd validated that the darkness inside me wasn't just my imagination. It didn't matter where it came from, or how it got there. It was there . . . and it was up to me to control it, not let it control me. I just had to be strong, be smart, and play safe. Find the release that did the least damage.

I'd stopped fighting, but I still drank, and I still fucked strangers. The darkness didn't come as often since that night I'd confided in Val, and deep down I knew that meant something. I just hadn't figured out exactly what.

It was because of Val that I wasn't a raging alcoholic. Somehow, he always knew when the darkness started to creep in on me, and he was there. I figured it was because he had his own secrets, and he understood.

"I'm just feeling a little restless is all." I set down the knife and met his gaze. "No big deal."

"Wanna talk about it?"

"Nothing to talk about, really. Like I said, just a little restlessness. Having nothing going on in my life makes me spend too much time in my own head." He really was a good man. "How'd you know anyway?"

His lips lifted in a small smile. "You only put this CD on when you're psyching yourself up for something."

"Well hell," I said. "It's better than grabbing a bottle, right?"

"Right you are." He stood and put his empty bottle on the bar. "Your mom called, said she'd been trying to get hold of you."

"I'll give her a call."

"See that you do." He gave me a look. "And remember, you can call me anytime, even if it's just cuz you need a kick in the ass."

My chest got tight and I couldn't speak. I nodded once instead, and Val nodded back.

I really was blessed.

The bar was packed that night and time flew.

I'd called my mom after my talk with Val, and let her ramble on about Ariel's wedding plans, my cousin's new baby, and an intern position in one of the city's top marketing firms she'd *heard* about. Yeah, more like she'd hunted down. No matter how many times I told her I liked my job, she never quit trying to find me something "better."

Whatever. I accepted that I'd never change her mind about following my own path.

A few drinks, plenty of flirting, and a complete lockdown on those pesky twinges of lonely had me feeling pretty damn good as I exited Risqué. It was my life, and I was living it the way *I* wanted.

Dave, the cocky young stud visiting Jack, was leaning against my car with his arms folded across his chest.

"It's my last night here," he said when I stopped in front of him. "I thought you might want to give me a going-away present."

A tingle of heat started low in my belly. I hadn't heard from Randy since getting back from Jamaica and my needs were riding me hard. Dave was pretty hot. Nice face, nice body, good sense of humor . . . and leaving town the next day. He'd be good for a quick fix, if nothing else. "Sure, hop in."

The drive to my place was short, filled with flirtatious one-liners flung back and forth. Dave's hand rubbed up and down my thigh as I drove and my temperature rose. When we hit a red light I turned and grabbed him by the shirt collar, pulling him in for a kiss. Our lips met, parted and meshed with the heat and passion only strangers can have.

Kissing a stranger—fucking a stranger, is hot. For me, the turn-on came from more than what the guy looked like, or who he was. It came from the fact that we'd never see each other again. I could be free with a stranger, as down and dirty as I wanted, as sweet or as slutty, and not worry about repercussions. Or judgments. Or gossip. It was an aphrodisiac, and by the time I pulled back from Dave we were both panting hard.

"Is it much farther?" he asked.

Instead of answering I put the pedal to the floor and pulled into the parking lot of my building two minutes later. Dave got the hint and didn't bother talking anymore. He smacked my ass when I went up the stairs ahead of him and pinned me to the wall on the first landing with a kiss.

His tall, lean body rubbed against mine as his hands ran down my back and fondled my ass. I started to lift my leg and wrap it around his waist but stopped myself and pushed him away to dash up the last set of stairs.

Dave caught up with me as I pushed the door open and we stumbled into my apartment together. The tank top I was wearing came off and I tossed it to the floor as I walked backward toward my bedroom, leading him along teasingly. His hands shook as he unbuttoned his shirt and belt, dropping his clothes on the floor where he stood. I eyed his pants and he understood. Reaching down, he pulled a condom from the pocket. When he came up, my skirt and panties were on the floor and he tackled me with a growl.

We hit the ground kissing and touching, hands everywhere as we rolled around on the floor of my living room. It didn't matter that we never made it to my bedroom; all that mattered was the feel of bodies rubbing together as we wrestled.

Dave tried to slow things down, to gentle me, but I wanted none of it. I didn't want gentle. I wanted hard and rough and passionate. Pushing against his shoulders I finally gained the top position.

I sat up, straddling him. "Put the condom on," I said.

Panting filled the room as he ripped the foil package and reached between us to slide it on. I lifted up, and got rid of my bra.

He froze, slack jawed and staring as I pinched my nipples and tugged on the piercings.

"You are so sexy," he said, his eyes glued to my every

movement. A shudder racked his body and I grinned. His cock was so hard it was flat against his belly.

"So eager," I whispered, trailing my finger over his cheek to the corner of his mouth. I played it over his mouth, dipping between his parted lips. "Do you want to fuck me, Dave?"

"Oh God, yes!"

"I'm not some sweet little girl, you know."

"I know." He panted the words out.

"Then do it." I gripped his shoulders and rolled over again, pulling him on top of me. Wrapping my hand around the back of his head I pulled him down on top of me. I pulled my finger out and kissed him. I sank my hands into his hair and pressed my body against him. My mouth opened and I shoved my tongue between his lips. He met me with fire and passion, his body rigid and straining against mine.

No more foreplay, no more teasing. I reached between us to grab his cock and showed him the way in. Once his thick head breached my entrance, he started to pump his hips. I planted my feet on the floor and moved with him, but it wasn't enough. "Don't be gentle, Dave. Fuck me hard."

"You asked for it," he said. Bracing his hands by my shoulders, he thrust deep and didn't hesitate. His hips pumped fast and hard, shafting me so deep it almost hurt. Pelvic bones crashed and my clit absorbed every shock with a cry of pleasure. I wrapped my legs around his waist, closed my eyes, and enjoyed the ride.

Dave didn't last long at that pace, and soon he was grunting. "Come on, sweetness. Come on."

I knew what he wanted, but I wasn't even close to coming. I was just enjoying the feel of his body above mine and his cock inside me. I tilted my hips to change the angle and gasped. That was it, right there. Dave started to adjust to my change and I grabbed his hips. "No, right there, baby. Don't stop."

Another grunt and he dug in. I moaned and grabbed my breasts, tugging on my nipples, pinching them until the pain shot through my body and made my pussy clench. Yes, there it was. "Yes, harder. Harder!"

He slammed into me and the pressure inside exploded. I caught my breath and absorbed the sensations that washed over me.

"Yes!" Dave cried out, his back arching as his cock hit home one last time before he collapsed on top of me.

I wrapped my arms around his shoulders and stroked his hair for a few minutes while he caught his breath. When he rolled off me I got up and went into my bedroom for my robe. I slipped the silk kimono on and went back to the living room, flicking the lights on as I went.

Dave was stretched out on the floor, naked and looking way too sleepy. I walked past him to the kitchen and opened the fridge.

"I have tequila. Would you like a drink?" I called out as I poured some over ice for myself. *Please say no.*

"No thanks, sweetness. I'm ready to crash now."

Crash? No that wouldn't do. I picked up the phone and walked back to the living room and flopped onto the sofa so he could hear me. "Yes, I'd like a cab please."

Dave's sleepy gaze snapped open at my words. His face went blank and he stood, heading for the bathroom as I gave my address to the dispatcher.

A minute later he walked back to the living room naked. "Thanks for that. I really should get going. My flight leaves early tomorrow."

"You mean today," I said.

"Yeah, today." He glanced at his watch and grinned before pulling on his clothes. "No rest for the wicked, right?"

I shook my head and chuckled. I remembered when it was a point of pride to stay up all night. My skin began to tingle and that being watched sensation rippled over me again.

Turning my head I walked slowly to the balcony and focused on the building across the street that housed some pretty fancy lofts. And I spotted him.

A guy alone, in the window directly across from me. Light spilled out from the room behind him, delineating his silhouette and leaving his face in the shadows. I didn't need to see his eyes to know they were on me, I could feel them. My nipples snapped to attention and my insides clenched in acknowledgment.

10

Just how much had the guy across the street been able to see with the lights out? Had he seen me fucking Dave?

Did I care?

Dave was behind me, his arms circling my waist and his lips nuzzling my ear. "Are you okay?" He kissed me softly, gently, as if to make up for his earlier roughness.

I turned away from the watcher and placed my hands on Dave's chest. "I'm fine. Thank you," I replied before taking his hand and leading him to the door.

He'd been just a fuck, barely even scratching my itch. But it would have to do for now.

When he was gone I turned out all my lights and sat down at the little table on my balcony. I finished my drink while I watched the silhouette across the street, hoping he would turn his light on and show himself. Adrenaline mixed with curiosity and arousal as I waited for what would happen next. Would he turn on his light and let me see him? Was it even a him? It had to be a him, the broad shoulders and straight torso were clear. I'd just convinced myself the watcher was a mannequin and my imagination was running away with me when it shifted, blending back into the loft.

Something that wasn't disappointment fluttered in my chest and I downed the last of my drink. The sun was starting to rise and I was ready for sleep.

I rolled out of bed around noon on Sunday and didn't bother to shower. The sun was bright and the air was already hot and humid. Not the best day to do yard work, but that didn't mean I wasn't going to do it.

Pulling on shorts and a tank top that had one of those flimsy built-in bras, I tied my running shoes up and went out to the yard, such as it was. Without one of my padded bras on, my nipple piercings were easily visible, but I didn't care. Some days a girl just had to go braless.

The place I lived in was an old apartment building that went condo five years ago. Only three stories high, there were four units on each floor occupied by a combination of newcomers and the same people who'd been there for the last twelve years. People like Manny and his wife who were settled and happy with their rent control, the occasional artist or student, and a few like me who wanted to help clean up the building. I considered my unit a worthwhile investment.

Which is why I'd stepped up when the last building manager was fired, and why I was willing to spend a Sunday afternoon mowing the lawn. I walked around to the side of the building and went through my key ring until I found the one that unlocked the little metal shed there. Inside I found a mower, rake, and all sorts of tools I had no need to ever use.

I wheeled the mower out and hoped it had gas in it already. Then again, if it didn't, I wouldn't have to cut the grass. I looked at the overgrown mess and sighed. It had been unattended so long I felt guilty. I'd promised Paul and the management company I'd do it, and I would. Besides, I wanted the place to look good when the new building manager showed up, so he'd keep it that way.

A couple of pulls on the starter, and the engine caught. I put my earbuds in, turned my iPod on, and started pushing. Sweat dripped down my forehead as I bopped along behind the mower, up the small yard, then down, then up, and on it went. The bag filled and I turned the machine off, dumped the bag in the Dumpster in back and strolled back to the front. The yard was over halfway done and I was feeling pretty good.

After wrestling to get the bag back onto the machine I stood up and spotted a guy walking up the other side of the street carrying a paper bag in one arm. There were lots of people walking around, but this one stood out. Over six feet tall with broad shoulders and slim hips, he moved with a grace and ease not often seen in big men. Sunlight glinted off his short dark hair, making it shiny and rich with highlights. He wore dark wraparound sunglasses but I knew he was looking right at me.

He was my watcher.

My nipples hardened and my sex clenched. It had to be him.

Frozen in place, I watched as he came closer, but he didn't cross the street. His head did turn, and his lips tilted up in a small smile before he turned right and entered the building across from mine.

It had to be him. But why hadn't he come and said hi? He had to know I'd seen him the night before. I'd looked right at him, or at his silhouette anyway.

Confused, I did what I did best. I pushed my emotions and mental musings aside and started the mower again.

Must keep busy.

The yard work was done, the hallways were cleaned, the garbage all taken out and a deep restlessness still filled me. Unable to sit still or concentrate on the novel I was working my way through, I jumped from the sofa and headed for Manny's apartment.

"I thought I'd take a look at your tap," I said when he opened the door.

He looked at the tool kit in my hand. "You going to fix it?"

"Maybe. But don't get your hopes up."

He opened the door wide and ushered me in. I hadn't lied earlier. I wasn't a handyman, but I did have a father who believed women should know the basics in home and car repair. Not only could I change a fuse and wire up a sound system, I could change the oil in my car, and flat tires were nothing to me. It wasn't my job to fix Manny's sink, but I was going stir-crazy in my apartment so I figured why not take a crack at it.

Manny chattered on in the background as I examined his tap. I installed new washers, and put some silicone around the joint where the pipes met beneath the sink. The whole thing lasted thirty minutes and I was back in my apartment, pacing, and thinking about my watcher.

How weird was it that he didn't freak me out? The urge to deliberately put on a show for him was strong, making my pulse pound and my pussy throb. I'd never really thought of myself as an exhibitionist before. Many other things, but never an exhibitionist. I wasn't really fond of opening up and feeling exposed.

But giving him a show would be all about the visual. It would be skin and movement, heat and desire, teasing and taunting. It wouldn't be emotional.

It was something to think about, and think about it I did when I stretched out in bed that night. Images of myself dancing naked with a stranger's hot eyes following my every move helped me find pleasure as my fingers danced between the slick folds of my sex.

11

isqué was closed on Sunday nights, and opened at eight the other six nights a week. Four of those nights a week I was the first person in—aside from Val, that is. But that Wednesday I worked the short shift, from ten 'til close.

I walked in just after nine and the place was still quiet, so instead of jumping behind the bar I headed to the corner booth where staff always lingered until things picked up.

"No fucking way!" Savannah Morris, one of the club's go-go dancers, shouted just as I got there.

At Savannah's outcry Callie held her right hand up, palm open. "I swear it."

"Swear what?" I asked, propping a hip against the side of the booth.

Savannah gaped at me. "She's never had a male-induced orgasm."

Ohhh, sex. My favorite topic of conversation. But first . . . I turned to the third person in the booth. "Good to see you, Joey. Show going good?"

Joey Kent was one of the best dancers at Risqué. So good that she only worked on a very casual basis for us now because she was part of a local dance troupe that put on seasonal shows. I'd only seen her two or three times all summer, and I'd missed her. She wasn't a close friend, but she was one of those people with a true-blue good heart, and it showed. Just being around her brought out the happy in a person.

"Summer run is over, and we start rehearsals for the winter show in a month, so I'll be around a lot more for a while."

"Nice," I said. Then turning to Callie I continued the previous conversation. "Never?"

"Never," Callie said.

Perplexed, I gazed at her. "How can that be when you're in love and all?"

Color flooded her pale cheeks. "I don't know. It's just never happened."

Savannah leaned forward. "Does your boyfriend suck in bed?"

"No!" Callie looked away from us and fiddled with the straw in her drink. "He's good."

"Good?" I asked

Joey shook her head. "Good isn't a great recommendation, sweetie."

Callie sniffed. "Good is good enough for me."

I was shocked. "How can you say that? Sex isn't supposed to

be *good*. It's supposed to be great, fantastic, and out of this world. It's one of life's basic pleasures. How can you settle for *good*?"

Joey and Savannah were nodding and Callie was chewing on her bottom lip. "I don't think he sucks. I think he's good, but how would I know? We've been together for three years and he's the only guy I've ever had sex with."

Joey and Savannah started babbling at Callie, throwing out all kinds of questions and advice and I sat back to take it all in.

"If he's not getting the job done, then you need to find a new man."

"But I love him."

Joey twirled the straw in her drink. "She doesn't need to get rid of him. Just take charge, Callie. Nothing makes a guy strut more than getting his woman off. Tell him what will do it for you and he'll be more than happy to oblige."

"I can't tell him what to do!"

"Why not? You don't need to give him step-by-step instructions. At least I hope to God you don't have to, or maybe you really should get a new man."

They all laughed.

"Just do the female thing," Joey said. Then she softened her voice and started sighing. "*Oh, there, baby. Yeah, just like that. No, deeper. Harder, faster . . .* Y'know, like that. Coach him."

I was laughing so hard tears were forming. To make matters worse, Callie's fair skin was flushed bright red and her eyes were about to jump from her skull. "I can't do that!"

"Sure you can," I said. "It's easy."

"No," she said. "I mean *I can't*. I don't know what I really like. I mean I like everything he does, it's just . . . not enough."

"What do you mean, you don't know what you really like? How are you supposed to tell him how to please you if *you* don't know what pleases you? What gets you off when you play with yourself? Do you like to play with your nipples or do you need clitoral stimulation?"

"Ohhh, there's nothing better than one of those little silver bullets." Savannah jumped in. "I'll always remember the guy who introduced those to me. His cock wasn't very big, but he made up for it in other ways."

"What's a silver bullet?"

Callie leaned closer to Savannah and the two proceeded to talk about toys. I turned away from them and focused on Joey. "So how are things with Mike?"

She grinned. "Great. Now that he doesn't work nights here anymore we have a lot more time together."

"And you're happy about that?"

Joey and I were a lot alike. As a dancer she always had men asking her to go home with her at the end of the night, but never out for dinner or a real date. We used to talk about how after being single for so long, we might get so set in our ways that a steady man would be more hassle than he was worth.

"Yeah, I am happy with that." She smiled and I saw the contentment in her eyes. "Getting used to having him around all the time was a lot easier than I expected. Great sex on a regular basis really helped."

I nodded. "It would, wouldn't it?"

"And you? How are things going? I heard you went on another beach trip?"

"Jamaica was good, and now life's back to normal."

She eyed me. "Nothing new and exciting?"

Well, some stranger has been watching me in my apartment, and I think I like it. "My little sister's getting married and I'm trying to help her find a dress. It's freakin' nuts."

The club had slowly been filling up while we talked and I could see a line starting to form at the front bar. Just then John, the bartender, looked up and our eyes met. It was time for me to get back there.

"Why don't you talk to Samair about one?" Joey said as I straightened away from the booth.

"About a wedding dress?" That got my attention. "You think she'd be interested?"

"Shit, yeah," Joey said as she stood up and removed her warm-up jacket. "Why wouldn't she? Especially if your sister has some unmarried friends who might need a dress in the future."

Beneath her light jacket Joey had on a strapless corset and miniskirt that I knew were custom-made by Val's girlfriend. They looked really good. Asking her about a wedding dress was definitely something to think about.

aturday was my normal errand day, and I spent it getting groceries, hitting the bookstore, and stopping by Samair's new storefront to drop off some pictures of Ariel to see if she'd take a crack at making a wedding dress in less than a month's time. By the time I got home late Saturday afternoon, I was feeling frisky and ready to shake things up.

I'm used to people watching me while I work, a bartender is just as much entertainer as drink master, and I had plenty of flair experience to keep people watching. But in the past week I'd started looking at any guys in the club that were six feet or taller, and wondering if they might be my watcher from across the street.

It was time to introduce myself.

As soon as the sun set that night I flipped all the lights in my apartment on, and began to dance, alone in my living room. Wearing a black button-up blouse and a flowing black summer skirt that swayed with my movements, I closed my eyes, let myself feel the music, and imagined him sitting right in front of me.

Raising my arms above my head, I started out like a belly dancer. I swayed, I twisted, I swiveled my hips and let my hands run down over my breasts and up my thighs, lifting my skirt and then letting it drop. The music filled my head and flowed through my veins as, with slow deliberate movements, I undid each button, one by one. The blouse hung open as I moved, my fingertips trailing over my bare skin, teasing me, teasing him. I'd enjoy giving my watcher a lap dance. Oh yes, I'd make him sit and watch while I moved above him and he couldn't touch. It would be delicious.

Sweat rose on my skin in the heat and I let the blouse fall from my shoulders to the floor. Still dancing, I let my hands play upon my thighs, lifting and dropping my skirt as I moved—flashing more skin. No, a lap dance would be too crude. I'd want to dress up in some fine lingerie and do the burlesque routine. The art of the tease is so much sexier than the crude bumping and grinding of modern strippers.

Although crude and raw certainly did have their place.

I dropped my skirt so I wore only my electric pink bra and thong set. Reacting to the change of music, I gave up the sensual tease and did some bumping and grinding against an imaginary lover until the urge to strip completely and dig out my toys was throbbing through my system. Then I opened my eyes and looked beyond my balcony and directly across the street.

He was there.

Without hesitation, I spun on my heel and picked up the piece of cardboard I'd written on earlier . . . and held it up for him to read.

12

555-6541

Excitement ripped through Harlan. She was giving him her phone number.

He set his camera down and stepped back from the window. The question was . . . why?

He glanced around the loft, seeing the images of her he'd already worked on. Should he call her? His gut clenched and he remembered the way she'd looked standing out on her balcony, lost and alone. There was no should or shouldn't to it. He couldn't *not* call her.

Lifting the camera, he zoomed in and reread the number. Where the hell was his phone? His worktable was a mess. It was an organized chaos though and he knew the phone was there somewhere. He just wasn't sure exactly where.

Muttering the numbers over and over, he shuffled some paint

tubes and brushes around, pushed aside an old canvas and finally found the phone beneath a dirty cloth that stunk of turpentine.

He punched the numbers into the phone and arrived back at the window in time to see her answer.

"You've been watching me," she said. And it wasn't a question.

"Yes."

"Why?"

Did he even know why? Sure, she'd been the muse that got him painting again, but it was more than that. He'd always been a people watcher, but he'd never taken it to this level before. He'd never *spied* on anyone.

"You're beautiful," he said simply.

"It's more than that, isn't it?"

She knew. This woman who was so innately sexual somehow *knew* that there was more to his watching than just a quick thrill. Did she feel the connection between them too?

"With some people." He paused, and she let the silence linger. "Yes, with you there's more to it. Your beauty is definitely there on the surface, but I think there's more to you than you show the world. You intrigue me."

Intrigue was a mild way to put it, but he didn't want to scare her off.

She'd gasped and he wondered if he'd freaked her out anyway. Would she hang up? Maybe call the cops on him?

But she didn't. Instead he watched her lean against the railing of her balcony as she spoke. "You like to watch." Her voice was better than he'd imagined. Husky, and just a bit rough, it sent a shiver down his spine.

He picked up the camera again. Without it, he could see her body fine, but the other night the need to see more, to examine her expressions and see the emotions dance across her face had found him digging through the closet for it.

With it he felt closer. Everything he saw through the lens was magnified. She became more than a female body. He could see the expressions that flitted across her pretty face, and the rigid way her nipples pressed against the material of her bra.

"I like to watch you." He watched then as she twirled a lock of hair and smiled.

"And do you like what you've seen?"

A chuckle rose from deep within. He shouldn't be surprised by her ready acceptance of him. He already knew she was special. The urge to tease her back was strong. "Most of it, yes."

"Most?"

"I liked watching you dance, and the sex the other night was nice too. You're wonderfully uninhibited. But my favorite was watching you ride that rubber cock stuck to the chair."

Her eyes rounded in surprise and her mouth formed a perfect O, but she recovered quickly.

"Big surprise there," she said with a laugh. "Do you stroke yourself when you watch me?"

"Sometimes."

"Are you now?"

"My hands are full right now with the phone, and the camera."

"Camera?"

"I dug it out of a closet for the zoom lens, so I can see you better."

"Would you be stroking your cock if your hands weren't full?"

Interesting that she hadn't asked if he'd taken any pictures. He thought about the question she had asked. He was hard, but there were times when a deeper pleasure could be had by waiting. "No, not right now."

He watched her pout for a moment, her lower lip thrusting out in a way that made him want to bite it.

Then she moved on. "Do you always use the camera?"

He smiled. "Not always. Sometimes I just like to watch your body move, but when I want to see more, to see *you*, I need it."

"Like now."

"Like now," he confirmed. "I can see you more clearly. Learn things about you."

"What do you see right now? What have you learned?"

"I can see your smile, and a bit of a flash that tells me your nose is probably pierced." His pulse beat faster. "The flush in your cheeks and your hard nipples tell me that you're enjoying this as much as I am."

Silence fell and he listened to her breathe. She sucked her bottom lip between her teeth and nibbled, and his gut clenched. The hand not holding the phone rose and she scraped her nails over a nipple in an almost subconscious gesture. She was such a sensual creature that he doubted she was even aware of doing it.

She finally spoke again, almost whispering into the phone. "What's your name?"

"Harlan."

"I'm Kelsey."

Pleasure washed over him. It was a simple thing, her telling him her name. But it solidified the connection that was growing between them.

"Will you continue to watch me, Harlan?"

He caught his breath. "Would you like me to?"

She left her balcony going back into her apartment. When she was in the middle of the room she turned and smiled at him. "Yes, I think I would."

Then she hung up.

Satisfaction unlike anything he'd felt in a long time rose up in Harlan. He'd never been a big believer in fate, but right then, he was convinced that it was somehow at work.

A people watcher by nature, he did it all the time. He'd sit in a park, or at the food court in a shopping center. He went to the movies and watched the audience, not the movie. As an artist, people fascinated and inspired him. He liked to watch them when they were unaware because it's then that there is no pretense. It's then that their true selves show clear.

He'd never gotten hooked on watching any one person in particular before. Even with Kelsey it had been an unconscious thing. She'd caught his attention when he'd been daydreaming at the window, chasing his muse instead of working. He'd seen her dance around before. He'd even seen her crying, but those times had never really touched him. She'd just been another person.

Until the afternoon she'd put a chair in the middle of her living room and proceeded to ride it with abandon. She'd seduced him that afternoon.

It wasn't just the sexual aspect of what she'd done that had hooked him; it was the rawness of it all. Her actions, her emotions, they'd been real, and deep. She'd *reveled* in her sexuality, and it had brought forth a primal response in him. He'd wanted her, but more than that, he'd wanted to worship and pay tribute to her.

He glanced at the canvas a few feet away from where he stood. He'd painted that day. He'd been in a slump since moving in to the loft and deciding to focus on his art full-time, but the piece he'd started that day was show worthy. And he had sketches of many more, all inspired by her.

Days after that first session, when she'd been hurting on her balcony, he'd wanted to comfort her. For the first time in years, emotion had stirred deep within him.

Kelsey touched him, and he couldn't walk away from that.

13

I woke on Sunday morning with thoughts of my personal watcher flitting through my mind. It was my lazy day, and my plan was to do nothing but read in the quiet peace of my apartment. I rolled out of bed and went to the balcony where I stretched out on a towel in the sun for a while. I'd yet to get a good look at him, my watcher that is, just silhouettes and that quick glimpse on the sidewalk.

Shit, I forgot to ask if that was even him I'd seen outside.

It was. When he'd looked at me, his gaze had felt familiar. It had to be him. He was a big man, and that pleased me. I liked big men. They made me feel feminine.

In concession to the heat, I wore nothing more than my bikini bottoms as I left my overheated patch of sun on the balcony to sit in my IKEA papasan chair and read my romance novel.

From time to time I'd feel eyes on me, and I'd bite back a

smile. Harlan. It was strange, the way that knowing he was there was almost a comfort. And instead of discouraging me from touching myself as I read the hot love scenes, the knowledge that he might see me was encouraging.

I wasn't being crude, or raw, but the brush of my fingertips on silk covered pussy lips, a little nudge against my piercing there or a tug on a nipple was normal.

Women often joked about how men couldn't watch TV without scratching themselves and I often wondered if I was the only woman around who couldn't read a romance novel without absently touching myself.

A tear leaked from my eye as I finished the last page late in the afternoon. Tossing the book on the floor I wandered my apartment for a bit, straightening things up, doing the few dishes in my sink, watering the one plant I hadn't killed yet.

Bored, I reached into the fridge and pulled out a bottle of Stoli. Pouring an inch of vodka into a glass, I held it as I paced. A minute later I was back for another shot as I eyed the phone and considered my options.

Ariel was busy with wedding shit. Dee might spend the occasional Sunday afternoon with me, but nights were her husband's . . . and a glance at the clock showed it was after seven already. Risqué was closed so I couldn't even go kill some time on the pool tables.

I could call Val and maybe he'd be interested in going to the gym, having a sparring match or something, but then I'd be taking up some of his alone time with Samair.

It was Sunday evening and all the couples would want to be couples, not friends.

Normally I like my own company. But sometimes my head was a bad place to be and I could feel the dark loneliness hidden there creeping forward. A look confirmed the bottle of vodka was still three quarters full and I stopped myself from pouring another glass. Instead I grabbed my gym bag and headed for the door.

An hour on the treadmill didn't do it for me. I spent another twenty minutes beating on the heavy bag, but it didn't help either. Restless energy was burning through me, the need to feel something other than alone pushing it along. I'd known when I'd brought Dave home last Saturday night he would be nothing more than a quick fix, and I was right. I needed a release.

As soon as I exited the door of the gym I had my cell phone in hand and was dialing Randy's number. "What are you doing tonight?" I asked as soon as he answered.

"You?" he shot back.

"Actually, I'll be doing *you*. My place in an hour."

I knew *he* watched as I strolled slowly around the living room. I pretended not to notice, but I was highly aware of the figure across the street, watching me through the open curtains as I waited for Randy to arrive.

Harlan had to know something was up just from my outfit, and I found myself hoping he was getting as turned-on by the thought of watching another show as I was of putting one on.

Randy was the first guy to respond to my singles ad on the Internet months ago, and soon after we'd shared our first drink together, we'd discovered that there was no romantic spark or connection between us at all. However, the way his eyes had lit up at my flirtatious comment about wanting a live sex toy of my own had started us on a different path. One we both enjoyed on a very casual basis.

Having Randy around had curbed my appetite for one-night stands with strangers. A bit. He wasn't a boyfriend, but he was a lover.

The buzzer announced his arrival and I went to open the door. I unlocked it and stepped back deeper into the hallway. Randy entered my apartment, closed the door behind him, and then stood there like a good boy.

Adrenaline pulsing through my veins, I began today's game, speaking from the shadows.

"Go take a shower," I commanded. "I want you to wash yourself everywhere, and don't come out until I tell you."

"Yes, mistress," he said with a small smile and headed straight for the bathroom.

I gave him a few minutes to undress and get under the shower spray. To keep myself busy I went back to the living room and did one last check on the toys I'd set out on the coffee table.

Sex was something I seemed to have a natural affinity for. A soul-deep craving that had always been with me, and made me a bit of a freak. If being the black sheep in my conservative family hadn't made me feel alone, my first couple of boyfriends, when I was younger, made it clear to me by telling me I was a *freak*, or saying I was simply too much, did.

I've always enjoyed sex, a lot, but I'd never been into anything too exotic. Before Randy it was just sex, mostly with strangers for an extra thrill—to give it that nasty edge I craved. When I was with a stranger I didn't have to worry about what he thought of my appetite for a little bit of rough. With strangers I didn't care if they thought I was good in bed, or if I pleased them. With strangers it was all about getting off, and nothing more.

But Randy showed me that I wasn't a freak. There were others out there who hungered for the more adventurous side of sex. He was the only guy to ever spank me, and *wow*, had that been a thrill. The best thing was that it worked both ways. Randy liked to be topped, and there were times when I really needed to be the boss.

Clenching my hands, I closed my eyes and took a breath to calm my racing heart before entering the bathroom to lean against the counter.

"Open the curtain so I can watch you wash."

The curtain slid back and a slight spray hit my skin, surprising me when it didn't sizzle on contact. Randy glanced at me and froze, his eyes widening and his cock jumping against his belly as he took in my outfit.

Running my hands over my latex bra and cupping my breasts, I smiled at him. "Like my outfit?" I turned slightly so he could see the way the thong bisected my ass, but his eyes were glued to my legs. Covered in silk stockings . . . and a pair of two-inch heels with an open toe and a strap around the ankles.

Very dominant-looking shoes. Shoes that made me feel sexy and in charge and made Randy drool.

"Randy," I snapped.

His gaze jumped to mine and he swallowed, his Adam's apple bobbing visibly. "Yes, mistress?"

"You didn't answer me. Do you like my outfit?"

Eyes on fire, he licked his lips. "Yes. Very much."

Randy, with his boyish good looks and lean athletic body, wasn't the type of man I was normally attracted to, but he offered me more than a pretty face or a hot body. He offered me the freedom of uninhibited play.

He absently ran the bar of soap over his chest and down his belly, then used his soapy hands on his cock and balls.

"Do your ass too. Make that little hole nice and pink and clean for me."

His eyes shone brightly as he bent forward and reached deep between his legs.

When he was sufficiently clean I instructed him to turn off the shower and step out so I could dry him off. I walked around him in the small space, toweling him off roughly. Tweaking his hard cock as it bobbed in the empty air.

"Follow me," I said as I turned to leave the bathroom. "On your hands and knees."

I walked to the living room and sat down on the couch. Randy crawled over to me and stopped at my feet. I noticed his eyes were glued to my shoes and wondered if he had a fetish he hadn't told me about. "You like my shoes, Randy?"

"Yes, mistress. They're very sexy."

"Kiss them."

He leaned forward and his hot breath skimmed over the top of my foot a second before his lips touched. He kissed the leather strap across the top of one foot and then the other. I watched as his tongue darted out quickly before he pulled back.

"Sit back on your knees."

I then placed my right foot on his left thigh, and my left foot on his right thigh. "Spread your thighs wide apart, and lean back on your hands." When he was in this posture I slowly began walking my feet up his thighs, and over his chest. And I wasn't gentle with the spikes.

Randy's cock swelled and the head turned a deep purple in response to the slight pain. A deep moan escaped his lips when the tip of my shoe brushed his chin. "Kiss my toes," I instructed.

His head tilted forward and he placed his lips on my silk-covered toes. He kissed and nibbled on them until I was fighting the urge to squirm in my seat. I'd never thought of my toes as an erogenous zone before, but he was so obviously turned-on by my shoes and feet that my insides started to churn.

"Enough," I commanded and he stopped immediately. "Using only your lips and tongue on my pussy, I want you to make me come."

Eyes bright with lust Randy slipped my shoes off reverently and placed them to the side. His fingers trembled as he skimmed his hands over my feet. He would've lingered if my impatient sigh hadn't warned him to do as he was asked.

His head snapped up and his hands trailed up my legs to spread my thighs. His hot breath whispered over my pussy lips and I tilted my hips forward, prepared to enjoy.

His tongue slipped inside me, and my feet inched their way up his spread thighs. His tongue circled my clit, tugging on the ring piercing the hood as my feet brushed against his cock. It didn't take long for Randy to figure out what I had planned, and soon all his attention centered on my clit.

My feet rubbed and stroked over his hard-on, his pre-come sticking to the silk covering them. Gentle pleasure rolled through me in waves as he worshipped between my thighs, licking everywhere, sucking and nibbling a bit until my clit came out from its protective hood. The jewel on my piercing rested against the hard nub and Randy began to work it until a lovely little orgasm washed over me.

"Sit back," I commanded when I caught my breath.

Randy immediately pulled back and sat straight, his buttocks resting on his heels, hands by his side, eyes shining bright. His true mistress had trained him well.

Well enough for a neophyte like me to enjoy his submissive nature.

I kicked him in the chest softly. "All the way back." I wanted him fully exposed to me, and to my watcher across the street.

Bracing his hands on the floor behind him, he leaned back, his cock thrusting up from the nest of blond curls. I made him watch, his eyes following me as I rolled one stocking down my leg, then the other.

When my feet were bare, I scraped my toes over his thighs, a thrill zipping through me when he shuddered at the light touch. I pressed harder, and he moaned. I nudged his warm balls with my toes and cupped his hot cock between my feet, and he whimpered, firing up my blood.

Randy's eyes closed, his head fell back, and his hips arched into my caress. I held my feet tight to him, pressing them in a way that had his cock thrust between the arches. "Make yourself come," I ordered.

Without hesitation, he began to pump his hips, his cock thrusting back and forth between my feet. Heat built up, and fluid eased out from the head. His panting breath was music to my ears, his whimpers and groans making my heart throb and my pussy clench. "Come, Randy. I want to see your cock jerk and come cover my feet."

With a final thrust of his hips his cock throbbed and twitched, come jumping from the tip as I pressed my feet together, squeezing him.

His chest rising and falling slowly as he caught his breath, Randy stayed exactly in the position I'd put him in. Until I lifted my feet and spoke. "Into the bathroom now," I ordered. "Get a damp towel and clean my feet."

He started to stand, but one look in my eyes and he started toward the washroom on his hands and knees, while I enjoyed the view of his tight buttocks and pondered how pretty they would look, pink from a nice spanking.

I wasn't a *real* Domme, but playing at one had its advantages.

* * *

hree hours later I was just getting into the *West Wing* marathon on cable TV when my phone rang. The late summer sun had set and my popcorn bowl had long since been empty so I got up from the sofa, and grabbed it on my way to the bedroom.

"Hello," I said without looking at the caller ID.

"Why do you always send them away?"

His voice sent a delicious shiver down my spine, and I smiled.

I'd been tempted to call him earlier and ask him if he'd liked the show, but I wasn't ready to let him know I'd been thinking about him. "Once we've both gotten what we wanted, why should they stay?"

"And you're sure you're getting what you want?"

"From my strangers? Yes." I crawled into bed, pulling the sheet up to my chin and snuggling down.

"What about what you need?" His voice had lowered.

"I'm getting exactly what I need."

"I don't believe you."

My heart skipped a beat. "Oh really? You think you know what I need?"

He chuckled. "I think I'm learning, yes."

Cocooned in the darkness, with only his voice and his words for company, I felt strangely safe. "And what is it that you think I need?"

"A firm hand, an open mind, a hard cock, and a loving heart."

My breath caught. I don't know what I'd expected him to

say, but I hadn't expected that. It was too close to what I dreamt about in my heart of hearts.

"What about you?" I asked, changing the subject. "What do you need?"

"I don't think I'm ready to share that with you just yet, Kelsey."

"Yet?"

There was a pause and I held my breath, eyes closed as I pictured him in my mind, framed by the windowsill as he looked into my apartment, into my soul.

"Yes, Kelsey," he said. His voice had dropped an octave, becoming rougher with his own emotion. "Yet."

"Oh."

"Sweet dreams," he said softly.

"I prefer my not-so-sweet dreams, thank you," I said, getting over my surprise and snapping back to my sassy self. "They're so much more fun."

His deep laugh echoed in my ears even after I'd hung up the phone and cuddled up to my extra pillow.

14

I was late. I fucking hated being late. Especially when I was meeting my mom.

Plus, it was Monday. And Monday mornings were just obnoxious, no matter what I was doing.

"Sorry I'm late, Mom," I said as I rushed into the restaurant and gave her a hug.

Charlotte Howard was nothing if not gracious, even to her daughters. "It's all right, sweetheart. I didn't expect you to be on time so I brought my wedding planner with me and I got quite a bit of work done while I was waiting for you." She was also the queen of the subtle guilt trip.

"Well, Mom, you know I work late nights and that I'll never be a morning person, so why did you want to have lunch at eleven? Who has lunch at eleven instead of twelve anyway?"

"I have another appointment at noon, with the florist for your sister."

"Of course," I said. "How are the plans going? Everything going to be ready in time?"

The waitress came and took our orders, smiling pleasantly when my mother told her to rush the order because I'd been late and now she was in a hurry.

"The plans are going very smooth. Lena is in charge of the bride's party and she would like if you could call her."

I sat there and tried not to fidget too much as she went on about the wedding plans. Don't get me wrong. I love my mom, and she loves me. I know she does. It's just that she's a complete girly-girl when it comes to romance, and the fact that one of her daughters was about to get married was putting her into hyper-drive.

And all the talk of weddings and family and toasts was starting to give me hives. When the waitress arrived with my smoothie, I took a big drink and my muscles relaxed just a bit.

My mom saw my slushy drink and the frilly garnish and frowned. "Sweetheart, you shouldn't be drinking so early in the day. Didn't you say you just woke up?"

"It's a smoothie, Mom. Made with yogurt and frozen fruit." And a shot of vodka for added flavor. Really.

Mom reached for her planner and started showing me pictures of the church, the hall, the cake design. When the waitress brought our meals and she was forced to put away the pictures she finally brought up her real reason for asking me to lunch.

"So what have you gotten Ariel and Miles for a gift?"

I bit into my pizza and used chewing time to think of something good. But I came up blank. "I don't know yet, Mom, but I still have a few weeks so I'm sure I'll find something."

Mom reached into her planner and handed me a typed-up list. "These are the stores they're registered at. You can go online and pick something."

I made a face and my mom frowned. "Kelsey, this is about your sister and her soon-to-be husband, not about your need to always be different."

"I don't always need to be different!"

She waved my comment aside and pointed her fork at me. "Don't get them gift certificates for matching tattoos or anything like that. Your sister is much more conservative than you."

Gift certificates for matching tattoos. That was a good idea. Or piercings. They could get funky and no one need ever know. Ariel was just adventurous enough that that might appeal to her, but I didn't know my soon-to-be brother-in-law well enough to guess what he'd think.

"Kelsey."

I faced my mom and tried to look innocent. "What?"

She laughed and I grinned. "That was a good idea, Mom. Maybe I'll get you and Dad the gift certificates for Christmas."

"Who's to say we haven't beat you to it? You think you're the only one in the family with a bit of a wild side?" she said with a wink.

The funny thing is, it wouldn't surprise me to learn my parents had matching tattoos. Both of them had a wicked sense of humor, even if Mom was too conscious of image and propriety to admit it.

We finished eating shortly after that and Mom rushed off to her meeting with the florist and I headed to the mall and the first store on the list she'd given me.

15

The shopping was hell. I couldn't find anything even remotely unique. My mom was right, sort of. While I didn't always have to be different, I did want to get my sister something special for her wedding, and somehow I just didn't think a toaster—even if it did cost eighty dollars—was special.

Frustrated with the whole thing, I swung by Dee's pub on the way home. She wasn't around when I walked in so I perched on a stool at the bar and ordered a beer.

Micky's was supposed to be an Irish pub, but it didn't resemble any of the pubs I'd been to in Ireland. It was all rich dark wood and high-back booths with shamrock green lampshades hanging over them. There was a dartboard in the back and a dozen different types of drafts lined up along the wood.

It was nice, but when I was in Ireland all the pubs I'd been in were slightly worse for wear, loud with either sports on the telly or live music. And they had only Guinness or cider on tap.

I'd met Jesse right outside a pub that I'd gone to for the music.

"Kelsey," Dee cried, tearing me away from my memories before they could get a good hold of me.

"Hey woman," I said when she joined me at the bar. "How you doing?"

"Good. What are you doing out and about this afternoon?"

I told her about lunch with my mom, and my subsequent efforts at gift shopping. "What was your favorite gift when you and Jason were married?" I asked.

"Honestly?" she asked.

"Of course."

"Jason's sister gave us a scrapbook she'd made full of pictures of us together. She must've tracked down everyone we knew because there were pictures in there from parties and things that I'd never seen before. I know it's sort of cheesy, but everything is digital these days. Computer slide shows and wedding videos and all that. The scrapbook had a great personal touch, and it's one of a kind."

I remembered Jason's sister calling me for pictures. I hadn't even asked what they were for; I'd just handed over some copies of my favorites of Dee, and what few I had of them both. It was a good idea, but . . . "Scrapbooking is so not my thing."

Dee laughed. "I'm sure you'll think of something unique. You always do."

She hugged me and went back to work. I sipped my beer and contemplated the whole wedding gift thing. I enjoyed dabbling in art, but crafts were not my thing. I always ended up gluing strands of my hair together or something equally idiotic.

"Wow, you look great in that outfit, but it would look even better on the floor of my bedroom."

I turned my head and stared at the guy who'd just sat on the stool next to me.

Shaggy blond hair that fell over one of his big brown doe eyes, and his lips that looked softer than a girl's as they spread into a cocky smirk. Mind you, the lips were the only soft thing on him. My gaze drifted down his hard body and images of riding him like a bucking bronco gave me a hot flash.

Young, dumb, and full of come. A silly saying, for sure, but it was the first thing that popped into my mind.

"Excuse me?"

He laughed. "Sorry about the cheesy pick-up line, but it *did* get your attention. Can I buy you a drink?"

The eagerness in his eyes had a certain appeal, and an afternoon of naked fun and games with a young eager stud would've appealed to me at any other time. But the earlier thoughts of Jesse and our connection that night in Dublin had brought thoughts of Harlan to mind. I'd yet to meet him, but the idea of dabbling with the young boy toy couldn't match the spark of excitement just thinking about my watcher caused.

A lightbulb went on in my mind and the spark turned into a bonfire. Hot blood swept through my body, pooling between my thighs. Right then and there I felt my pussy lips thicken and my juices start to flow. If my watcher had been nearby, I would've thoroughly enjoyed a little tryst with the young blond.

But Harlan wasn't around, and that made me feel strangely let down. That, however, didn't mean I couldn't give said boy toy something to think about the next time he jerked off. After all, he'd tried. It wasn't his fault I was craving something more than he could offer.

I finished my beer and set the empty glass on the bar before turning to him. Behind him, I could see Dee standing in the doorway to her office, watching us. Leaning in real close, so that my breath feathered the curls over his ear, I whispered, "I'm sorry to say it's not a good time for me. Otherwise I'd be happy to take you home, tie you to my bed, and ride you hard for the next twenty-four hours."

I patted him on his tight little ass and slid off my bar stool. Feeling powerful and sexy, I headed out of the pub, his sputtered requests for my phone number echoing behind me.

A riel say's you're the go-to girl for all things naughty and wild," Lena said when I called her from the bar that night.

I laughed. "What did you have in mind?"

"Well, as you know, I'm in charge of your sister's bachelorette party, and I want it to be fun and sexy without being tacky. You know what I mean?"

"Right. No drinking from penis cups or balloons taped to her shirt that say 'Poke me while I'm still single.'"

There was a snort and gurgle on the other end of the phone before Lena laughed. "Cripes! Next time I'll know better than to drink while I'm talking to you. Pop is not meant to go up my nose!"

"Sorry." I bit my lip. Ariel and her friends were no innocents, but I'd have to remember not to be so frank with them.

Lena's husky chuckle echoed over the phone line. "No worries. You summed up exactly what I was talking about. I have some ideas for fun things, like I've hired a psychic to come in and offer readings for the girls, but I'm, um, having trouble with the sexy aspect of it all. Plus, I was hoping you could maybe get us a deal on the private room at Risqué since you work there?"

"Do you have a firm date for the party?"

"Two weeks from this Saturday. The week before the wedding. And did your mom tell you she wants to be at the party?"

The worry in Lena's voice made me laugh. "No, she didn't. But I wouldn't worry about it. My mom might be a bit of a snob about education and career, but she's pretty relaxed at parties. I doubt she'll stay for the whole thing anyway."

I did some quick mental math and told Lena I'd look into booking the private room. Ideas started swirling and I mentioned the caterer who'd worked Samair's fashion show earlier that year. Ambrosia specialized in naughty but tastefully done events of any size.

"Oh, that sounds good," she said.

When Lena started asking if there should be a stripper or gift bags for the guests I had to roll my eyes. A small line was starting to form in front of John, the other bartender, and I had to get back to work.

"Listen," I finally said, "you're helping Ariel with a bunch of other stuff, right? Why don't you let me handle the details of the party?"

"You'd do that?"

"Sure. Not the guest list. You handle that part because I really don't know any of your friends. But I'll book the room and figure out the entertainment and stuff. Sound good?"

"It sounds wonderful, Kelsey. Thank you!"

We said a quick good-bye and I went to work beside John. I'd talk to Val later about the room and a few other ideas I had.

B ooking the private room at Risqué was no problem, and Val, good guy that he was, let me have it for free. Which gave me a bigger budget for the actual party.

"You're such a sweetheart," I said as I gave him a hug.

"Brat," he said lovingly as he smacked me on the butt lightly and pushed me out the door at the end of the night. "Don't let that get around."

I shoved the caterer's phone number in my purse and climbed in my car. During the drive home I came up with all sorts of naughty things to do at a bachelorette party and I had to keep reminding myself that this was for my sister, and not me.

I t was the last weekend in August and Mother Nature was in a mood. I'd rolled out of bed on Sunday morning and gone to the gym only to quit halfway through my workout because it was just too damn hot.

Hot and *humid*.

The pressure built in the atmosphere as the day wore on and the restlessness inside of me matched it. It was one of my days off and my first mistake was that I wasn't doing anything. I'd tried reading, my favorite way to spend a quiet day, but my mind wouldn't settle down. Yet, there was nothing special on my mind either. I tried watching a movie, but even Bruce Willis couldn't hold my attention for long.

Bored, I picked up the phone and dialed Dee's number.

"What are you up to this afternoon?" I asked as soon as she answered.

"Laundry," she said with a laugh. "Jason's watching the football game then he's going to grill us up some steaks. Want to come over for dinner?"

Yeah, hanging around watching the married couple smile and coo happily at each other was just what I wanted to do. "I don't think so. Thanks for asking though."

We talked about Ariel's party for a couple of minutes before I hung up. I paced my apartment some more, driving myself just a bit nuts until, finally, I stretched out on the sofa and closed my eyes. I concentrated on my heartbeat, breathing in through my nose, then out through my mouth. In . . . out . . . as thunder ripped through the air, echoing the restlessness in my soul.

A storm was coming.

Thunder continued to roar and with a loud crack the skies opened up and rain poured down. Jumping from the sofa I went out to my deck and stood in the rain, staring at the still bright sky.

Within seconds it was over and I stood there, drenched, but feeling somehow cleansed. Feeling Harlan's eyes on me, I glanced across the street. He was there, watching me through the rain. All week I kept imagining that someone was watching me, even at work—looking at every guy who was six feet or taller with dark hair and wondering if it was him.

I stared back at the image in the window, the sudden twinge of awareness in my sex making it clear that simply putting on a show long distance for this guy was not enough anymore. I wanted it up close and personal. I wanted skin to skin, panting breath and screaming orgasms. Spinning on my heel I went inside and reached for the phone.

I gave a brief thanks to caller ID, and dialed.

"Hello, Kelsey." His voice was warm, almost affectionate.

"Are you busy tonight?" I asked.

"Not with anything special."

"Would you like to see a show?"

He hesitated and I could almost hear his brain shifting gears. He thought I was asking him on a date. "I meant, would you like me to put on a show just for you?"

"I'd like that very much," he said, his voice deeper than it had been.

Adrenaline rushed through me and I bounced on my toes.

"Be here at ten," I said, then hung up before I could change my mind.

16

All primed and pretty, I strolled through my apartment dimming lights and lighting candles as I sang along with Nickelback's "Animals." Hard-hitting and raunchy, it was the perfect song for what I had in mind.

My heart pounded as I plumped the pillows on my bed and made sure the condoms were within easy reach. Then I went back to the kitchen and stared at the bottle of Stoli. It was there, right in front of me, but the urge to drink had fled.

I was standing there, leaning against the kitchen counter when the buzzer sounded and my pussy clenched. I pressed the button that would let Harlan into the building and went to unlock the door. I stood there, listening for his footsteps, and opened the door before he could knock.

"Hi there," I said.

More than six feet of solid muscle stuffed into jeans and a

navy blue T-shirt filled my doorway. Harlan stared at me and my heart went pitter-pat while my hormones danced a jig to the beat.

His eyes were blue. Bright blue. And they roamed over me with an intensity that was almost disconcerting.

Unable to hold his gaze, I let my own run over him. It was my first real good look at him, and I was trying hard not to drool.

His hair was darker than it had looked outside, but it was so thick and rich my fingers itched with the need to touch. Dark skin stretched over features that were strong, raw, and masculine. The light scent of spice that clung to him told me he'd shaved recently, but stubble still rode his jawline, and probably always would. Muscles that were not built in the gym rippled with the slightest of motion and every construction worker fantasy I'd ever had flashed through my brain.

Harlan was no pretty boy, but he was panty-dropping hot.

Without saying a word I stepped back and waved him in, closing the door behind him. "Would you like a drink?"

He glanced at the bottle and glass clearly visible on the kitchen counter. "No, thank you."

Nice manners too.

Squashing my nerves I reached out and took his hand. "I'm glad you came."

A small smile lifted the corners of his lips and I got a strange swoopy feeling in my stomach. "I am too," he said simply.

"Follow me?"

He nodded and I led him into my bedroom.

The strategically arrayed candles cast a flickering light over the bed, but left the corners of the room in shadow, giving it a cavelike feel that I found comforting and erotic at the same time. The darkness surrounded us and welcomed the side of me that I only let strangers see.

Turning to Harlan, I reached up and put my hands on his shoulders, pressing him back until he sat in the chair I'd positioned at the foot of my bed. "Your seat, sir," I said with a saucy wink.

His lips twitched and his eyes sparkled. "Thank you, ma'am."

Reaching down, I covered his hands with my own. "Watching only, Harlan. Until the show's over."

"And then?"

His question hung between us as I started to sway to the music. "And then you'll fuck me until I can't walk tomorrow."

Moving back, my eyes slid closed and I ran my hands over my body. They glided smoothly over my hips, belly, and breasts as I started to move. I'd imagined giving him a lap dance, and I wanted it to last.

"Open your eyes," he said.

I did, and looked right at him, cocking a brow in question.

His eyes gleamed out of the shadows. "I want you to know who you're dancing for."

The heat in his gaze fired up my blood, and it rushed through my veins. I kept my gaze on his as I reached for the hem of the satin camisole I'd put on just for him. Lifting it slowly I pulled until it was over my head, and I was naked from the waist up.

When he didn't immediately look down, I brought a hand

up and sucked on my fingertip, then trailed it down over my neck and chest until I was circling a rigid nipple. His gaze followed my finger and a shiver ran through me when he licked his lips. I stepped closer, hips still swiveling in a slow bump and grind, my hands cupping both of my breasts.

I tugged on the bejeweled hoops in my nipples and gasped at the sensation that shot to my groin. "Do you like my jewelry?" I asked.

"Very nice," he said. "Almost as pretty as the rosy nipples they adorn."

I dipped forward, then moved back again and let my hands drop to my thighs. Bending my knees I exaggerated the bump and grind, lifting my skirt slowly, then dropping it. Spinning around, I looked over my shoulder as I gave him my back. I did the same move as before, bending sharply at the waist and flashing some ass before I straightened.

A low growl rumbled through the room and my sex clenched. I'd barely started my teasing and already the tension in the room was getting to us both. With little fuss, I slipped my hands beneath the elastic of my skirt and pushed it to the floor. It was time to really turn up the heat.

I sat on the bed directly in front of him and slid my ass back until I was leaning against the pillows. Looking directly into his eyes, I let my hand cup and fondle my breasts, fingers pulling at my nipples until I was panting. Then my hands drifted across my soft belly and over my trimmed patch of curls. Bending my knees up, I spread my legs wide for him.

I was completely naked and open to him, and he was fully

dressed, sitting as still as a statue. My gaze ran hungrily over the bulge at his crotch and I licked my lips. "Will you open your pants for me? Let me see how much you like my show?"

He didn't hesitate, undoing his belt and jeans smoothly and pushing them down his hips until his cock was free. Long and thick with a clear ridge riding up the underside to the shiny head, it bounced lightly against his belly. Oh, yeah, he enjoyed the sight of my wet pussy framed only by my bare legs.

The sight of his hand wrapped around his shaft, as his eyes fairly glowed with desire, had my pulse pounding. It was a hard choice: Did I want to watch him stroke his cock in that almost absentminded way, or did I want him to concentrate on watching me?

Sliding a hand between my thighs I watched as his gaze followed my every movement. My juices flowed faster and I slipped a finger between my pussy lips and into my hole. A second finger quickly joined the first and I fucked myself while he watched.

His own hand picked up speed, matching mine and making the head of his cock an angry deep purple as trickles of liquid squeezed out the tiny hole.

Another low growl echoed through the room when I pulled my hands away from my pussy and reached under the pillow. "Don't worry, baby," I said softly as I pulled out my pink jelly cock from its hiding place. "I'm not done yet."

I fondled the phallus, my eyes locked with his as I licked up and down the fake cock, wetting it and teasing him at the same time. Desire burned in his gaze and seared my soul.

This guy was dangerous, the heat between us fast becoming addictive.

Placing it between my thighs I spread my slick pussy lips with my fingers and played the toy around my clit. Slipping the fake cock into my sex, I began to thrust it, slow and steady, while frigging my clit with a fingertip at the same time.

A moan escaped as my inner muscles tightened and my hips started to push against my hands. I frigged my clit harder and fucked myself shamelessly. Moans filled the air and I couldn't tell if they were Harlan's or mine. I closed my eyes, really getting into the way it felt, not just putting on a show anymore.

"Look at me!" he growled, a tightly leashed tiger in my bedroom.

My eyes snapped open and I stared at him. Hunger flared bright in his blue eyes, the flames calling to me. Urging me to touch and be touched, to let myself get burned. I groaned and bit my lip. Oh, how I wanted him. I wanted that big thick cock of his shoved so deep inside me that I screamed.

"Come for me, Harlan," I begged.

His gaze snapped to mine and his mouth opened soundlessly.

"Please," I said again, panting as everything inside me tightened. "Come for me. I want to see you."

At that his body jerked, his hand squeezed and pumped faster as a low groan echoed through the room and jets of liquid burst forth. The sight of him coming sent me over the edge, and my own hips pushed harder against my hands shoving the vibrator deep inside my hole as my insides spasmed and pleasure over-took me.

When I came back to reality the first thing I noticed was the silence. The music had turned off.

Taking a deep breath and laughing softly I opened my eyes to see Harlan watching me, an unusual expression on his face.

17

W ow," I said.

"Yeah." Harlan nodded. "Wow."

Unsure of how exactly to proceed, I gently removed my vibrator and put it on the bottom shelf of the nightstand. The tissue box there caught my eye and I pulled a few out. Two steps and I was at the end of the bed, on my knees in front of Harlan. "Let me clean you up," I said softly.

He held out his hand and I wiped it clean with one tissue, and then kissed the palm. It was the first kiss between us, and our gazes locked.

Tearing my gaze from his, I looked straight ahead and skimmed a tissue over his cock. Little pieces began to stick to him and without thinking about it, I spit on the bundle of tissue in my hand, and proceeded to wipe him clean.

Then I realized what I'd done.

Horrified, I froze, eyes squeezed shut. I'd been so comfortable with him, so into the connection between us, that I hadn't thought twice about what I was doing.

Well, the best way to deal with shit was straight-on.

I opened my eyes and glanced up to see what Harlan had thought of my uncouth behavior. His lips had split into a wide grin and his belly was starting to shake from holding back his laughter.

Relaxing, I grinned up at him. "What? Didn't your mother ever spit on a tissue and wipe your face?"

"I am *so* not thinking of my mother right now."

As if to prove this, his cock started to swell. Amazing. I'd basically spit on him, and he was getting hard again. I was in love.

My gaze dropped to his groin and my hand reached out to touch again. "Yummy."

He pushed my hands away and zipped up his jeans. "That's enough, little girl."

I heard the playful note in his voice and my smile grew bigger. "Don't tell me you're shy?"

"Not shy, darlin'. Just not sure you're ready for me yet."

Surprised laughter jumped from my lips and I stood up, hands planted on my still naked hips. "Oh, really?"

"Yes, really." He stood too, towering over me. "We'll talk about it tomorrow."

My heart did a slow roll and thump at the promise in his eyes. *Wow.*

Really.

I swallowed and stepped back to put some space between us.

Harlan buckled his belt while I tried not to run and lock myself in the bathroom.

When his shirt was tucked in again, he looked down at me. His expression gentled and he lowered his head. My breath caught in my throat and I froze when his lips brushed over mine tenderly.

"Thank you," he whispered.

"Um. You're welcome," I said when he straightened again.

"Can I stay?"

That shocked me.

What shocked me even more than his asking to stay was the way my own head bobbed up and down in answer to his request.

I was used to kicking men out once I came, and he was the one who'd pulled away and done up his pants when things had started looking up again. Why did he want to stay?

Why was I letting him?

He put his hands on my shoulders and moved me backward to the edge of the bed. Lifting the sheet, he waved me in, then let it cover me before stretching out on the bed beside me and gathering me in his arms, spoon style.

"Harlan?"

"Shhh," he murmured. "Go to sleep."

There was a tall, dark, and delicious man in my bed, and I didn't know what to do with him. He'd completely thrown me for a loop.

Closing my eyes, I breathed deep, inhaling the slight spice

scent of him. Warmth surrounded me and my muscles turned to mush, dragging me into a serene slumber.

She had green eyes. Not hazel, not gray . . . green. A deep shade—hunter green. Yeah, that was it. And it suited her. Intense, dark, and very unique.

Harlan lay there and wondered at the events of the night and the emotions that were already growing within him. He closed his eyes and inhaled the heady scent of the woman in his arms. Peaches and sex. That's what she smelled like.

His dick twitched in his pants and he bit back a smile. He was definitely hooked.

Kelsey was all woman, not afraid to show it. Her invitation to come over had been unexpected, and surprising. He'd have bet money she was perfectly happy keeping him at a distance, but there was no way he was going to be happy with that now.

No way either of them would be.

The way she'd taken charge from the minute she'd opened the door until he'd tucked her in had impressed him. It was silly to be disappointed in her show.

No, not her show. She was beautiful and watching her would always be amazing, but he'd been hoping for a bit more of . . . *her*. There were definitely more layers to her than she showed. He sensed a certain wildness within her, and he wanted to get to know *her* better, not just her body.

The intelligence in her gaze and the sense of humor that was never far from the surface proved he was right. She had more to offer than the pure "come and get me, big boy" persona she carried around like a shield.

A shield.

Oh yeah, she definitely used her raw sexuality to protect herself. Not that it was an act; she truly was a sexual creature and didn't just behave like one for effect. Of that he had no doubt. But she did seem to hide behind it.

As much as it was a shield protecting her, it was also holding her back. He sensed the untamed need in her that wanted to get out. She was naughty and wild and dirty . . . but she wasn't letting completely loose.

The thought of her being completely open with him robbed the breath from his lungs. She would be such an untamed beauty. She'd have no match.

Slipping from the bed, he stood at the edge and looked down at his sleeping beauty. He memorized the way the lock of hair caressed her cheek, the way her lips parted slightly in sleep, the curve of her shoulder and the swell of breast that was visible at the edge of the bedsheet.

Brushing a fingertip over her soft skin, he turned and set about blowing out the candles in the room before leaving. Determination settled heavy in his gut. He was going to make it happen. He was going to bring forth the true and complete Kelsey, and make her his.

Five minutes later he was in his own loft, standing in front of a blank canvas. He didn't sketch out the image in his mind first; he didn't need to. He just focused on his mind's eyes and let the brush flow over the canvas.

18

ometimes, between dreaming and waking, I find the ultimate pleasure. A sure hand that knows exactly where to touch me, how to touch me, and the whispered words that make my heart, and my pussy, swell.

In that perfect time between sleep and wakefulness a hand creeps between thighs—my hand. In search of pleasure, but in no hurry. I don't spread my lips crudely and begin diddling right away. I just sneak a hand down there and let it lie against my core.

After those first few minutes, which give me comfort, my fingers begin to roll side to side. Arousal uncurls slowly in my belly as my pussy lips thicken and my clit stirs to wakefulness beneath them . . . and my mind floats on the same fantasy every time.

It's not my hand down there. Instead, I'm waking up next to

the man who shares my life. The one who knows just how to touch me, how to reach me.

The one who accepts me and all I am.

Only that morning it was Harlan in my fantasy. It was Harlan's hand between my thighs. I jerked up in bed, slapping a hand to my forehead.

What the hell?

With a grumble I crawled out of bed and stomped to the bathroom. I didn't bother turning the light on, I just twisted the taps until the water was running and climbed in. I bit back a shriek at the initial icy blast, but it did the trick. I was awake, and no longer thinking Harlan was my dream man.

Crap!

I turned the hot water up and steamed myself clean before turning the shower off and toweling myself dry. I should be in a great mood. I'd had a damn good time putting on the show for Harlan, and a good night's sleep. But I wasn't. My insides were all jittery and adrenaline was pumping through my veins. I didn't have a clue what the hell I'd started.

Dry, and still naked, I went to the kitchen and grabbed an energy drink from the fridge. Resisting the urge to add a shot of vodka to it to calm myself, I stared at the clock.

It was early. Not even nine o'clock yet.

God, I couldn't even remember the last time I was asleep before midnight. Harlan was a pretty potent guy, he hadn't even touched me and I'd been putty in his hands.

You're not ready for me, he'd said. What the hell had he meant by that?

I snatched up the phone and dialed before I thought twice. Dee answered on the second ring. "Kelsey?"

"Hey, sweetie," I said, keeping my voice light.

"What's wrong? Why are you up so early?"

I bit my lip. I'd called her for a reason. No time to button up now. "I need you to tell me again that fucking a guy the night you meet him isn't the way to start a real relationship."

"Kels!" Dee's exasperation was clear in her voice.

"What?" I snapped defensively. "Sometimes it just can't be helped. And I didn't really fuck him . . . it was more of an 'I put on a show for him' type of thing." *And now I'm sure as hell not going to tell you how we met!*

"Start from the beginning," she said.

Now that I had her attention I wasn't sure how much to tell her. Sure, she was my best friend and she knew I wasn't innocent when it came to guys—that I had casual lovers and one-night stands instead of boyfriends and real relationships—but I was feeling vulnerable, like an idiot. Part of me worried that if she knew how far I was willing to go for satisfaction, she might judge me.

Sure we both worked in the same industry, and she understood how easy it was to love people and hate them all at the same time, but she worked in a pub, not a nightclub. And she was married, and settled. She hadn't been part of the single lifestyle for a long time.

And if she judged me . . . and found me lacking I wasn't sure I could take it.

"Kelsey? Are you still there?"

"I'm here."

As if she knew what I was thinking she spoke with a firm voice, tinged with love. "Spill it, girl. You know you can tell me anything."

"Ah, it's nothing." I gave my head a shake. "There's a guy who lives across the street from me, a really hot guy, and I think we have some sort of connection. Or at least I thought we did, and I'm a bit worried that I might have fucked it up last night when I invited him over and masturbated for him."

I held my breath waiting for her reaction.

"You masturbated for him, and then he left?"

"Yeah."

"That's a new one, even for you."

What did *that* mean? "Yeah, I guess."

"See, this is exactly what I meant. If you didn't want to be single, you wouldn't do things like that. You'd go for coffee or to dinner, like normal people."

That hurt. "What? I'm not normal?"

"And this morning you're thinking you might want a relationship with this guy?" A car honked in the background but Dee carried on without answering me. "Are you freaking serious?"

"You're driving, I should let you go."

Frustration clear in her voice Dee said, "I'm not driving, I'm sitting on the fucking freeway which is down to one lane because of an accident. So take my mind off of it, tell me what's special about this guy."

"Nothing's special," I lied. "I don't know what I was thinking, forget I mentioned it at all." No way in hell was I going to tell her he'd been watching me *Rear Window* style and I felt like we had some sort of kinky connection.

That wouldn't be *normal*.

"You sure?" she asked.

"Yeah. It was an erotic adventure, nothing more."

A heavy sigh echoed over the phone line. "You and your adventures."

Silence hung between us for a few seconds. It never used to bother me when people didn't understand the things I did or my choices in life. Now it did, and *that* bothered me.

Whatever.

"Yeah," I said with forced cheerfulness. "I should let you go, you're on your way to work and I think I'm going to head back to bed."

"Okay, girl. If you're sure. I should get off the phone anyway, the traffic is starting to move again."

We said our good-byes and I hung up, not feeling any better.

I did my hair and layered on the eyeliner before going to my room to dig through my dresser drawer for something to wear. Ten minutes later I wore my swishy black skirt and a white tank top with black tribal-like tattoos along the neckline.

I'd always had a thing for art, and tatts were certainly a form of art I appreciated. Yet, I'd never gotten one. The thought of something so permanent on my body was too unsettling. Sure I had piercings, but they were dual-purpose. For beauty and pleasure. And they could be removed at any time. The same couldn't be said for tattoos.

So for a while I did the next best thing, I picked up some clothing paints, and started hand painting my own clothes. It wasn't the same as having real tattoos, but at the same time I could be more daring. After all, big black tribal tatts along my collarbone and chest would not look good when dressed for a wedding.

Mind you, if I ever found a design or symbol I knew I'd never tire of, I'd probably find a place to get it inked in and fuck looking good in a fancy dress.

I'd really enjoyed the painting, and had even briefly considered creating my own business around it. Vancouver was full of creative arts people, and I'd sold several hand painted pieces to friends and coworkers at the club. But in the end, I'd decided that just because I was good at it, didn't mean it was the right career move for me.

Now I painted clothes as gifts occasionally, and for myself, but that was it.

With thougths of gifts and fancy dresses in mind I called Ariel and told her I was picking her up for a quick shopping trip.

An hour later, I sat at the curb in front of Joe's Pizza and watched Ariel say good-bye to someone inside and then head toward me.

If you looked beyond the clothes and makeup, you could tell

we were sisters. Cut from the same cloth, so to speak, with fine black hair, green eyes, and similar builds. But that was where the similarities ended. Ariel was an accountant and bookkeeper for several small local businesses and liked to dress in professional skirts and slacks, button-up blouses, that sort of thing. I was the pierced bartender who liked to wear skimpy black clothes, drink, and tell dirty jokes.

Ariel kept her hair in a short bob, her makeup minimal, and always had a smile for everyone. She was cute, and sickeningly sincere. It was hard not to love her, especially when I knew she'd do anything for me.

"You're up early," she said when she climbed into my car.

"It's ten thirty. I'm usually up around now." If *around* meant in another hour.

"Up maybe, but not dressed, out the door, and looking somewhat human. No, this is not the norm for you, my sister. What's up?"

"I have a friend I want you to meet," I said as I pulled away from the curb and headed toward Samair's new storefront just off King Edward Drive.

Her voice rose an octave in excitement. "A man?"

"No!" I snapped in surprise. "What would make you think that?"

"I don't know. Something's different about you this morning." She narrowed her eyes at me and I concentrated on the road.

After a moment of silent scrutiny she spoke again. "There *is* a man, isn't there?"

Was there? Was Harlan really a man in my life?

Something thumped against the inside of my rib cage in reply. My heart. Okay, so he was in my life, but for how long? I had no fucking clue what was happening between us. Just the idea that something *was* happening was enough to make my pulse race and my palms sweat. However, like Val had taught me, I needed to be strong, and that meant not hiding . . . even from myself.

"There might be," I said cautiously. "I just met him, and it's a pretty . . . unusual situation, but yeah, I think I like him."

Yeah, way to jinx yourself, Kelsey.

"Unusual how? He's not someone you picked up at the bar is he? You know that will never last. Those guys like Kelsey the party girl bartender, they don't even care about getting to know you."

"No, he's not from the bar. Look, I'm not sure exactly what the hell is going on, so I'd rather not talk about it, okay?"

"Okay." A slow grin spread across Ariel's face and she sat back in her seat, looking smug.

That was too easy.

Traffic was minimal and finding Samair's storefront was relatively simple. Parking would've been a bitch but Samair had said to go around the back. As I drove up the alley the silence in the car made me finally snap. "What?"

"I didn't say anything," Ariel replied.

"You don't have to. I can feel your brain working from over here. So just say what you have to say." I turned off the car and opened my door to get out, talking as I moved.

Ariel followed. "I've just never seen you so worked up over a guy before."

"I'm not worked up. I didn't even say anything about him!"

"That's just it, Kelsey. You've never been shy with me about your men before. In fact, you usually delight in shocking me with your stories." I pulled open the heavy fire door and we entered the back of Samair's shop. We were in a small corridor and Ariel continued to talk as we walked. "The fact that you don't want to talk about this guy means he's special."

"Who's special?"

We'd reached the end of the corridor and Samair was standing there with a grin. "The hallway is like a megaphone, I could hear everything. Who's special?"

I groaned and fought the urge to stamp my foot on the ground. "No one is special. My sister is just making nothing into something. Samair, this is my sister Ariel Howard, soon to be Ariel Harrison. Ariel, meet Samair Jones, designer extraordinaire. She's got some sketches for your wedding dress I want you to check out."

The two women exchanged greetings while I glanced around the shop. Even though it was my first time there, I was pretty familiar with Samair's work. When she and Val had first gotten together, she'd held an exotic lingerie show at the club that had made me drool. I'd purchased a corset that night, one that looked great, and felt great even after a shift behind the bar.

The woman had talent.

"I have the sketches set up over here," Samair said, leading us over to the far corner of the room.

Obviously her work area there was a drafting table, a computer desk, and a long worktable filled with various fabric samples.

"Before we get started, do either of you want something to drink? Coffee, tea, diet soda?"

Ariel accepted a tea and I shook my head. When the pretty blonde went to make the drinks, Ariel turned to me.

"I can't afford a custom-made wedding dress," she hissed. "Are you nuts?"

"Relax. Samair is a new designer, and Val's girlfriend. She's willing to give you a really good deal if you'll spread the word about her."

"Oh."

Her brow furrowed and I reached for her hand. "What? If you don't like what she's come up with don't worry about it. There's no pressure here, Ariel."

"It's not that, but the wedding is coming up fast. What if I do like what she suggests, and can afford it, but she can't make it in time. I'd be heartbroken." She straightened her shoulders, her lips firming. "We should leave now."

I shook my head. "Get a grip, Ariel. That's the stupidest thing I've ever heard."

She looked at me, eyes wide and panicked for a split second. Then she took a deep breath, and excitement quickly replaced trepidation. "You're right. It will all be okay. This is awesome."

Okay. My sister was seriously stressed.

Samair came back and started showing us the sketches. I was quickly bored by all the talk of styles and fabrics and other wedding crap so I quietly left them alone and wandered the shop.

It wasn't fancy, but it was clean, and Samair's products were as drool-worthy as I'd remembered. I noticed that she had some ready to sell, and they were priced a lot lower than the custom-made stuff from the show she'd done at Risqué.

Two hours later we left the store happy. Ariel had a dress on order, I had a new lingerie outfit I couldn't wait to show off, and Samair had an invitation to Ariel's bachelorette party.

19

When I got home from work that night the light was blinking on my phone, so after stripping down and washing up I dialed in to check for messages.

"Hi, honey. Ariel called and told me about her dress and I just wanted to say how wonderful it was of you to arrange that for her. And to see if you've bought her and Miles a gift yet. Don't leave it to the last minute, Kelsey. Your sister would be very upset if you forgot. Maybe I should just pick one up for you? Would you like that? Call me back, sweetheart."

Like Ariel would care if she didn't get the gift on the day of. They weren't going to open any until they got back from their honeymoon anyway. I grimaced. I did need to find them a gift though.

The voice mail clicked off and I settled onto the sofa with the latest Jack Reacher thriller and a cup of tea. Just as Jack was walking into a room full of big bad mercenaries the phone rang and I jumped three inches. "Fuck!" I stared down at my lapful of tea, thankful it was only lukewarm by then.

It rang again as I was removing my wet shorts and I reached for the phone without looking at the caller ID.

"Hello?"

"How are you doing tonight, Kelsey?"

My just-steadying pulse jumped again at the sound of Harlan's deep smooth voice and was off to the races again. Leaning against the wall, I took a deep breath. "I'm doing good, Harlan. How about you?"

God, I sounded so stiff and formal, but I couldn't help it.

"I've been thinking about you," he said.

My knees went weak and my brain blanked. I banged my head on the wall. *Get a grip woman!* I was like a freakin' schoolgirl with a crush. This was a man who'd seen me do some very adult things. A man who I wanted to do some very adult things *with*.

Heat unfurled low in my belly and spread throughout my body, causing tingles in all the right places. Yes, adult things, sexy things. My confidence returning, I breathed deep. "And what have you been thinking?"

"That I want to get to know you better."

"You could've gotten to know me a lot better last night, but you left."

"You looked like Sleeping Beauty so I didn't want to wake you. Instead, I was thinking you should have dinner with me tomorrow."

"Dinner?" He was asking me out? Like a *normal* person.

"Yes, dinner. As in food and drinks, conversation and good company." Humor laced his voice and I snapped upright, an embarassing thought occurring.

I marched over to the patio and looked over at his loft. The lights were out, but that didn't really mean anything. "Are you watching me right now?"

"No."

Thank God he hadn't been witness to my weak-kneed girly-girl moment. "What are you doing?"

There was a small pause and some rustling sounds. "I'm in bed."

"Be still my heart," I said without thinking. "Would you like some company?"

A low chuckle rumbled in my ear and I turned away from the window, heading toward my room. I put some clean shorts on and I was ready to go.

As I stepped into my room Harlan's words put a stop to my plans. "Not tonight, greedy girl. I didn't sleep at all last night, or today, so I'm going to crash. I just wanted to make a date with you before I did."

Confusion, mixed with disappointment, made me a bit snappish. "Sorry, I can't do dinner tomorrow night. I have to work."

"Before you go to work then. I'd like to see you again, Kelsey."

He wanted to see me again? "Okay, not dinner, but drinks will work. You know where Bart's Martini Bar is?"

"Yes."

"Meet me there at seven thirty. The after-work crowd will

have thinned out by then, and I'll have some time before I have to be at work."

"I'm looking forward to it. Sweet dreams, Kelsey."

"Oh no, I like my not-so-sweet dreams, thank you." He chuckled and something fluttered in my chest. "Good night, Harlan."

All day long I waffled on my plan. Part of me wanted to listen to all the advice Dee had given me over the years and be the good girl—just go and have a drink and some conversation with him before I went to work. But the other part of me, the part that was never willing to settle, wouldn't let go of the fantasy once it had entered my head.

"Baby did a bad bad thing . . ." I sang to the image in the mirror the next evening. An hour with the curling iron had given me a just out of bed tousled look that framed my heart-shaped face. Artful application of makeup had my eyes looking slanted and my lips full and pouty. A quick swipe with some clear gloss and I was ready to go.

"Fuck it," I said to my reflection. "He wants to get to know me, he's going to get to know the *real* me."

Adrenaline pumped through my veins as I locked my apartment door and headed down the steps. With the curly hair, and clear lip gloss I was more pin-up girl than goth girl and it suited my purposes well.

The drive to Bart's was less than ten minutes, but it felt like forever. By the time I got to the bar, my panties were damp and my nipples were so stiff they ached.

A glance at the clock on the dashboard showed it was just after seven thirty. Harlan should already be there.

Bart's was a small brick building with a flat roof and opaque windows that let passersby catch just a glimpse of action on the inside. There was a parking lot on one side of the building and a rare books store on the other. It wasn't my usual hangout, but it was a perfect fit for my plan.

Hips swinging to the music in my mind, I sashayed into the place and stopped just inside the door. *"Baby did a bad bad thing."* Oh yeah, I was about to do a bad bad thing and it was going to feel so so good.

The place wasn't empty, but it wasn't full either. About half of the horseshoe-shaped booths along the wall were occupied, a few of the tables, and half of the long bar. A pretty decent selection of men to chose from, but no Harlan.

A tingle danced down my spine and my nipples throbbed. Turning my head slowly, I saw a lone man seated at a small round table with his back to the wall. Our eyes met and warmth flooded my system. He was here.

Tearing my gaze from his I walked right past Harlan and went up to the bar. I gave the three men closest to me a quick once-over then asked the guy on my left to buy me a drink.

He turned his body toward me with a polite frown. "Do I know you?"

I arched a brow and licked the corner of my mouth teasingly. "Does it matter?"

Realization dawned in his eyes and he smiled, his perfect teeth gleaming. "No, not at all. What would you like?"

I ordered a vodka martini. "Are you having a good night?" I asked the guy next to me.

"It's getting better." He held out his hand. "I'm Sam, by the way."

"Hi, Sam," I replied and glanced over my shoulder to see Harlan watching me closely. "Would you like to tell me your favorite sexual fantasy?"

"Um." I'd stumped him.

The bartender set my drink in front of me and took Sam's money. When he left, Sam had regained control of his motor skills. He leaned forward and spoke in a doubtful voice. "Are you offering to make it come true?"

"Maybe." I sucked the olive off the little sword and gave him a slow smile. "If it matches one of mine."

Sam was not a dumb man. He glanced around the room, looked me over, and then he spoke again. "One of my favorite fantasies is sex with a beautiful stranger in a public bathroom. How about you?"

"No." I shook my head. "The bathroom would be too obvious." And Harlan wouldn't be able to watch.

But like I said, Sam wasn't a dumb man, and now that I'd planted the idea in his head, he was eager. "The parking lot? My car?"

"Why don't we move to a booth? So we can talk about this some more?"

Sam's eyes widened, then he nodded. "Of course."

20

There was an empty booth about five feet from where Harlan sat near the back, so I chose it. I slid in first, and then Sam slid in next to me. "Why don't you come a little closer, Sam?"

When he was settled I dropped a hand under the table and put it on his thigh. Excitement raced through me at the thought of what I was about to do to a perfect stranger.

"I'm not going to let you fuck me, Sam," I said softly. "But I would really like to stroke you off. Does that appeal to you?"

"Here?" he croaked.

"Here." I moved my hand up his thigh until I was cupping his erection through his pants. "And now."

His Adam's apple bobbed as he glanced around the bar. We were fairly secluded, but it wouldn't be hard to get caught.

"Sam?" I toyed with his zipper.

"Yes," he said and pressed up against my hand. "Do it. Please."

Triumph roared through me as I unzipped his pants and freed his cock. Hot and hard, it wasn't huge, but it was a handful.

I smoothed my thumb over the tip, spreading the liquid that was already leaking out. Sam's hands twitched by his side and I bit back a laugh. "Just put them on the table, Sam. Then lean back and relax. Let me do all the work. I just want to feel you throb and grow in my hand. I love the feel of a man growing beneath my touch."

Wrapping my fingers around him, I watched him as I began to stroke. Up, down, squeeze at the base and twist a bit on the upward pull. Neither of us spoke as I worked on him. Sam's breathing picked up and my pulse matched the throbbing in my hand. It was so exciting, misbehaving in such a way. I almost wanted to get caught.

Sam tensed beside me and I looked up to see him looking straight ahead; panic and arousal clear as he saw a body moving toward our booth.

"S-s-s-top," he stuttered. "Someone's coming."

"Shhh, it's okay." I tightened my grip and pumped faster as I saw the six-foot-something of solid muscle that was approaching. "He's a friend. He likes to watch."

Harlan slid into the booth, all dark hair, dark skin, and bright blue eyes that were full of appreciation, and something else, as they roved over my face before dropping to my hand. "Hey, naughty girl. Having fun?"

"Definitely."

A choking sound came from Sam and his cock swelled within my grasp. Harlan slid closer to me, so close that the heat of his thigh pressed against mine and I shivered. The image of my other hand dropping beneath the table and stroking Harlan's cock at the same time flashed in my head and my inner muscles clenched. Oh yes, this was so bad, and so good at the same time.

"Reach beneath the table, Sam," I whispered. "Slide your hand under my skirt and feel how hot you've made me."

Sam's eyes closed, his hands clenched, and his body stiffened as he came, soaking my hand. My own arousal spiked and I moaned, rolling my hips and pressing my thighs together until a hot hand touched my bare leg and slid smoothly under my skirt.

My eyes snapped to Harlan.

Our gazes locked and I spread my thighs, opening for him eagerly. My pulse raced and a small moan escaped when his finger slid beneath the elastic of my thong and rubbed along my slit. He played for a second, spreading the wetness and watching me fight for control, which I almost lost completely when he found my clit.

My back arched and my thighs snapped shut, trapping his hand as his finger flicked my button back and forth. "Yes. Yes!" I cried from between clenched teeth.

I wasn't even aware of Sam leaving the booth. When my body stopped shuddering I only had eyes for my watcher.

After handing Kelsey a napkin to clean her hand off, Harlan leaned back against the padded booth and took a deep breath.

Part of him was angry, and part of him was so fucking turned-on he couldn't see straight.

Just when he thought he was on the right path with Kelsey, she took a left turn.

He twisted toward her, stretching an arm along the back of the booth to keep from touching her again as he watched her carefully. Where to start?

"Can I buy you a drink?"

Her lips twitched and she batted her eyelashes. "Is that your way of asking if I'll stroke you off next?"

"Nooo," he said slowly. "It's my way of asking if you'd like a drink, and some conversation. After all, it is what I came here for."

Surprise skittered across her face and was gone so quick he wondered if he imagined it.

Kelsey straightened and flashed him a sassy smile. "Sure, I'm always up for a drink. What would you like to talk about?"

He waved the waitress over and they ordered their drinks. A martini for her, and a soda and lime for him.

"You don't drink?" Kelsey asked as soon as the waitress stepped away.

It was a common reaction and he couldn't resist. "What do you think I'm going to do with the soda?"

"Drink it." She rolled her eyes. "But I meant alcohol."

"No, I don't drink alcohol."

Curiosity sparked in her gaze but she didn't dig further. Instead, she put her arms on the table and leaned forward, plumping up her cleavage and tilting her head toward him. "Did you enjoy the show?"

"I always enjoy watching you," he said, keeping his tone neutral.

"You don't sound very convincing."

"Does it matter to you if I enjoyed it or not?"

"That's a strange thing to say."

Instead of watching the way she postured or twirled a lock of her hair with her finger, he watched her eyes. They sparked lively, but she kept a tight rein on herself. "And you didn't answer the question."

The waitress arrived with their order and Kelsey sat back in the booth. When they were alone again, she smiled, and spoke confidently. "I enjoy having you watch."

An invisible bubble settled over them, enclosing them in their very own space. "Did you know him?"

She met his gaze. "No."

"Is that the thrill for you?"

"That's part of it." She grinned, and shifted closer. "But it's more than just the fantasy of a stranger, or even of a public place. I've thought about doing this exact thing plenty of times, I've even come in here and had a drink with the intention of doing it. But I've never had the nerve to follow through."

"Tonight you did."

"Yes."

"Because I was here?"

"Definitely," she said and leaned close, putting her hand on his thigh. "I know I should've been freaked out when I found out you were watching me, but I wasn't. Do you think that's strange? That this thing between us is strange?"

"If I say it is?"

She laughed and his heart kicked in his chest. She really was something.

"If it is, it is." She pointed a finger at him and grinned. "But remember, you're the one who started it all."

"Yes," he said. "Yes, I did."

Their gazes locked and neither spoke for a moment. Neither needed to speak, something *was* happening between them, and they both knew it.

"Are you mad?" she asked finally.

"No."

"Disgusted? Turned off?"

He took her hand and guided it from the table to the hard-on pressing against his zipper. "Does it feel like I'm disgusted or turned off?"

Color blossomed on her cheeks and her lips parted, her tongue peeking out. "It feels like you're angry."

He quirked an eyebrow at her. "Really?"

She shook her head, her fingers moving, cupping and measuring him through his pants. "Not this. This feels delicious. But . . . I feel like you're mad at me for doing what I did with that guy."

Breath rasping in his throat he moved her hand off him. He'd told her he didn't want to be jerked off under the table and it had been the truth. "I'm not mad. Disappointed, yes. Mad, no."

"Disappointed," she said. She pursed her lips and looked away, and Harlan felt like he was on the verge of losing her. "I'm a thirty-four-year-old woman at the height of my sexual peak, Harlan. I have fantasies to experience, some of which include things I'm only comfortable doing with strangers."

"Look at me, Kelsey." He hooked a finger under her jaw and pulled her face back around. "I'm not disappointed because of what you did. I'm not that man. I'm confident in myself and not threatened by watching a woman I find attractive with another man. What I am disappointed in is the fact that you'd rather play games than get to know each other."

Confusion swirled in her beautiful green eyes for just a moment, and then she pulled back. "You had the chance to get to know me better last night, and you said no."

Surprise ran through him. She'd felt rejected when he'd asked her out instead of inviting her over for a fuck!

He shook his head. Women. Really, every time he thought he had a clue, they proved him wrong.

Following instinct, he moved his hand from the back of the booth, cupped her head, and pulled her close so that they were only a breath apart. "Do *not* think I don't want to fuck you. You and I are going to end up in bed together again soon, and I promise you, the next time you won't get *any* sleep. But first, I just want to share a drink, talk, and get to know you. Do you think we can do that?"

A slow, sensual smile spread across her lips and her eyes sparkled. She leaned in and pressed her soft lips to his, stealing his breath.

"So, what do you do for work, Harlan?"

"I'm an artist," he answered automatically, fighting the urge to pull her onto his lap and give the whole bar a show. "That's why I have a very lenient schedule, which is good for getting to know women with wacky schedules like yours."

"An artist?" she said. She ignored his comment about schedules, but her cheeks flushed and he took that as a good sign. "That's so cool. What's your medium?"

Excitement colored her voice and he wondered at it. "I play with charcoal but my passion is oils. Are you an art fan, Kelsey?"

"Anything creative really." She shrugged, and glanced away. "I envy anyone who can write, paint, sculpt, or even take a decent photograph. It must be awesome to be able to create something out of nothing like that."

"Did you ever want to be an artist?"

"I've dabbled with sketching and painting a bit, but I wouldn't consider what I did art. It was just a hobby for a while." She looked like she wanted to say more, but then she blinked real slowly, and when she looked at him again her eyes were shuttered and her lips curved in a saucy smile. "I think posing for an artist would be more fun. Would you like me to pose for you?"

"Who's to say you haven't posed for me already?" He wiggled his eyebrows suggestively.

Kelsey laughed and flirted outrageously with him for the next hour as they talked, and Harlan fell hard.

She'd fascinated him from afar, but up close and personal she was bewitching. As she regaled him with stories of crazy happenings at the nightclub he just watched her perform. She smiled, she winked, she tossed her hair and laughed in all the right places.

Kelsey Howard appeared to be completely open, but as time went by he realized it was all on the surface. She was a shadow of the vibrant and raw being he'd seen when he was watching her on her own. She thought she'd put on a show for him with that stranger, but he knew the real show was when they were alone, and not talking about sex.

He saw it then. His way past her emotional shields was to play on her physical ones. They say the way to get to a man was through his stomach, and right then Harlan realized that the way to get close to Kelsey was to use her open sexuality.

She finished her drink and he slid out of the booth, holding his hand out to her. "Can I walk you to your car?"

They exited Bart's and he reached for her hand, entwining their fingers. It was a small thing, but it felt right.

They got to her car and she looked around the near empty parking lot. "I can't see you driving a smart car, a VW Bug, or a bright red Corvette. Where's your car?"

"I walked."

She leaned in to him and put a warm little hand on his chest. "Too bad I have to go to work or I'd offer you a ride."

His dick jumped in his pants at the promise in her gaze. A ride in her car wasn't the ride she was referring to.

Pulling her close he bent down and kissed her on the cheek. Her skin was so soft and the sweet scent of peaches filled his head, making him want to nibble on her. Hell, he really wanted to do more than nibble; he wanted to drag her inside and eat her up whole.

Ahh, fuck it.

His arms went around her and he lowered his head laying his mouth over hers. He didn't bother being gentle. One hand cupped the back of her head and he thrust his tongue between her lips and tasted every inch of her mouth. It was a carnal kiss full of heat and desire and the need to get closer. He breathed in her scent, tasted her flavor, and thrilled at the way she melted against him.

Strong little fingers dug into his shoulders and her tongue fenced with his. Heaven, she tasted like heaven, and he wanted to never stop. No other woman had ever affected him the way she did. One simple kiss and he was ready to make her his.

Taking a deep breath, he fought for control and pulled back slowly, pleased with the dazed look in her eyes. "Thank you," he said.

She licked her lips and hummed, still leaning into him. "You're welcome. Again."

He had to get out of there, fast. If he didn't leave soon, he'd lose it and jump her there and then. The little witch would probably love a semipublic fuck. Something to think about. *Later,* he told himself.

Instead of pushing things further, he clamped down on his desire and pressed a quick hard kiss to her swollen lips. "Have a good night, Kelsey. I'll call you."

He squeezed her hand before letting it go and turning on his heel.

Prepping the bar was way too easy and I floated through it with my brain constantly wandering back to my date with Harlan and the things he'd said.

Images of him buck naked between my thighs filled my head. Him over me, under me, behind me. Fuck, the images were so hot that my hands were trembling and I was actually starting to sweat.

He hadn't been pissed at me for making another man come right in front of him. Shit, he'd been excited by it. Sure, he'd wanted to have a better date with *me*, but he hadn't walked away when he'd seen what I was doing.

Excitement that I might've found a man who'd finally accept me in all my raw glory ripped through me.

For the first time in a long time, hope lifted my heart.

21

Once last call was done and the nightclub was empty the staff members came to get their "staff drink" as I finished wiping down my bar. The dancers, the bouncers, and DJ Rob were the first up, their job ended when the customers were gone. When Callie finished wiping tables she did a quick cash-out, and with a superior grin, handed over her envelope in exchange for a Zombie.

Earlier in the night we'd run out of Heineken and instead of sending the porter I'd gone to the cooler to grab a case myself, and caught Callie fucking one of the bouncers. I'd given them both a verbal warning; break or no break, they couldn't do that shit in the beer cooler.

Callie had taken the warning with a barely hidden grin and had proceeded to bounce around like a bunny rabbit on steroids, full of smugness because she'd finally experienced out-of-this-world sex. I was the last person to judge, but part of me had been disappointed in Callie, preacher of love.

I ignored the staff table and finished wiping my bar down. Grabbing my own cash drawer, I headed upstairs to the office.

"Hey, Kelsey." John, the bartender who normally worked the bar downstairs with me, had worked the VIP bar that night. He held out his cash drawer for me as I approached. "Take this in for me, would ya?"

I stacked his cash drawer and cash-out envelope on top of mine and he waved at the doorman at the front entrance and shouted, "Hold the door, Steve."

"Not sticking around for a drink?" I asked. John was one of my favorite coworkers. He had a bachelor of science degree, but he preferred bartending to working in a lab or teaching.

"Not tonight." His grin said it all.

"Got a girl waiting?"

He grinned. "She's in the car. You know sex trumps drinks every time."

As long as it's not in the beer cooler. "Have a good night," I said and made my way to Val's office.

"Aside from Callie and Chris in the cooler, it was a good night," I said and set everything on Val's desk.

"Sales?" he asked without taking his gaze away from his computer screen, which was full of motorcycles.

I recited the night's totals and he smiled. Val had almost lost Risqué once, and he'd sold everything to hang on to it. Including his dearly beloved Harley Davidson motorcycle. With the end of summer nearing, bikes would be going on sale soon. "You find the one you want?"

He glanced at me, eyes bright. "Oh, yeah. And I should be able to bring her home next month." He closed the browser on his computer and pulled the cash drawers in front of him.

"How does Samair feel about you riding around on a death machine?"

His harsh features softened at the mention of his girlfriend and he chuckled softly. "She's fine with it. She calls it 'the biggest vibrator ever.'"

I laughed. "Maybe I should get one myself."

"Don't you dare!" He cringed. "You'd get yourself killed inside of a week."

"What! You think a woman can't handle a machine like that?"

"Some women, sure. You? No. You're too much of a speed freak, adrenaline junkie."

"I am not."

He cocked an eyebrow at me. "How many speeding tickets have you gotten in the last month?"

"Only one."

He shook his head. "How many times have you been stopped, only to flirt your way out of a ticket this month?"

Damn. "Three."

"I rest my case."

"Fine." I pouted. "I'll just ask Karl to take me for a ride next time I see him."

Karl Dawson was Val's best friend. He was big, blond, and dangerously sexy. Not necessarily good-looking, but *sexy*. As in, pussy clenching, ask me to do anything and I'll do it sexy. And being a sexual Dominant in the local BDSM community, he had plenty of women who would do *anything* for him, and say please at the same time.

"Lara might have something to say about that."

Oh, yeah. He also had a girlfriend now. She seemed nice enough, and I might've even liked her, if Karl wasn't so obviously in love with her.

I crossed my arms and thrust out a hip. "Ruin my fantasy, why don't you."

Val laughed and waved his hand at me. "We both know you and Karl would never be a match. Now, get out and go home. Relax and find your own vibrator."

I bowed at the waist. "Yes, sir. That's an order I can follow."

He balled up a piece of paper from his desk and threw it at my retreating back.

That night, as I was brushing my teeth and getting ready for bed, my phone rang. Knowing it could only be Harlan, I grabbed it and went to sit on the balcony.

"How was your night?" he asked.

I thought about it all.

"Long, but good." A sigh pushed out of me. "Y'know, I love my job. I really do, but sometimes I get so tired of being a babysitter to the young and intoxicated—and that's just the staff."

He chuckled and my blood warmed. He'd set a chair near his window and I could see him sitting there, his feet propped up on the windowsill as we talked. We didn't talk about anything special—just jokes, favorite movies and authors, living in Vancouver.

Talking was nice, and very relaxed. We watched the sky turn pink and the sun rise, and then said good night. I crawled into bed as the birds outside were chirping their greetings to the new day and fell into a dreamless sleep with a smile on my face.

It was supposed to be my Friday off, but John called early in the afternoon and begged me to cover his shift so he could go to a concert. Always a sucker for a begging man, I agreed to work it for him.

However, that didn't mean I could cancel all my other plans for the day and I had an appointment with the caterer for Ariel's party.

Lacey Morgan greeted me with a big smile and an enthusiastic wave when I got to the little coffee shop where we were meeting. "Kelsey! I'm so glad you called me for this. I know we can come up with something perfect for your sister."

I sat down with my iced mocha and grinned at the woman across the table. She oozed positive energy and I was completely comfortable. "I'm sorry this is such short notice, Lacey, but I just sort of took over handling the party for my sister's maid of honor. Lena's helping Ariel with other wedding stuff, and I love coming up with sexy ideas and shit, so here I am."

"No problem. The gig that really launched Ambrosia for me was a bachelor party—with no strippers allowed—so this sort of thing holds a special place in my heart."

I'd though about hiring one of the male cage dancers to work the room, but Ariel was a lot more conservative than me, so I wasn't exactly sure how that would go over. She had a naughty sense of humor, but a bumping and grinding hottie might be pushing the boundaries of her comfort zone. "How did you do it?"

"A naked woman on a table with sushi . . . and a few extras for dessert." Lacey winked and wagged her eyebrows.

"Sounds erotic, but not something my sister and her friends would go for. Even if it was a naked man instead."

Lacey leaned forward. "You have to understand something, Kelsey. I'm a caterer, I love food in all its many forms . . . but party planning is not my forte. However, when you're starting a business and a big client wants the whole package, you find ways to give it to them, which was the case with that bachelor party. I honestly think my lack of traditional training or knowledge with party planning helped. I didn't need to think outside the box because I had no idea what was *in* the box! So, food themes I'm good with, and I'm very open-minded and have a lot of contacts for all things sensual and erotic, but the actual planning and detail stuff, I'm not good with."

"No problem, I've got plenty of experience planning events

at the bar." I chuckled and shook my head. "Val told me you were mainly a caterer, but that you were also ambitious and *sensually creative*."

Her lips tilted up at one corner. "I like that."

I laughed. "It is a great description."

Our gazes locked and in that moment I felt a connection snap into place. I'd met Lacey briefly when she was working Samair's party at the club, but right then, sitting across from her in that little café, we became friends. Instinct and years of sizing people up quickly told me that Lacey had experience with things not always of the norm—in her personal life and her professional. She gave off an erotic vibe that had my radar humming.

Lacey Morgan was a woman who definitely had a sexual nature that at least flirted with the more adventurous side of things. I could feel it. I also got the impression that if I wanted to step into her playground, she'd welcome me. But, as much as part of me wanted to know more, an even bigger part wasn't ready. There was hunger to get closer to the edge with my sex games, but deep down, I didn't want to do it alone. I wanted someone to take that journey with me—a man who would accept that wicked dirty part of me, and revel in it.

Giving my head a shake I focused on the project at hand. "I think I have an idea, for the party."

I sucked some of the iced mocha up through the straw and waited for Lacey's reaction.

"Great." She smiled. Even though we'd never said a word about anything other than the party, she knew I was changing the subject. "Let's hear it."

"Lena already hired a psychic to come in and give readings. Y'know . . . who your true love will be and all that sort of thing, and that made me think of an erotic carnival type thing."

"Go on."

"Well, my mom will be there, and my sister's not as . . . adventurous as some, even though she likes to think she is. So, instead of rides at the carnival, we can set up games, that sort of thing. Maybe hang curtains or use screens or something and separate the room into three or four areas. A general area for mingling and food and drinks and maybe a spanking booth, a toy chest booth or game of some sort with sex toys as prizes, and I can probably get one of the cage dancers from Risqué to give dancing lessons or striptease lessons or something like that."

"What a fucking fantastic idea!" Lacey cried.

The breath I hadn't even known I was holding rushed out and I grinned. "Really? You like it? You can work with it?"

"For sure!" Excited color flushed Lacey's cheeks and she waved her hands about as she threw out more ideas. "We can do cupcakes decorated to look like body parts, and erotic chocolates and something with monster hot dogs." She waggled her brows.

I loved her! We brainstormed a complete range of ideas from raw and raunchy to sensual and sexy. Lacey Morgan was a kindred soul, completely open and full of adventurous ideas. Soon we had more ideas than we knew what to do with, and Lacey sent me home with a list to consider, and narrow down.

That night, before my shift, I'd called Dee to see if she'd be into helping plan Ariel's party. If she didn't want to, that was fine; I'd still love to have her there with me at the party for a good time. It had been way too long since we'd been out dancing. I went into Risqué a little early and found Val and Samair half-dressed and cavorting in his office, which made recruiting *them* to help me plan the logistics of the party very easy.

The good mood I'd been in since my visit to Bart's with Harlan was gone by the time I got home from work that night. There were hundreds of people who'd had a great time at Risqué, but I was not one of them.

Too many drunk idiots with stupid pick-up lines. Too many young kids who thought the world revolved around them. Staff members with petty arguments and silly dramas made me feel like I was back in high school again, only this time I was the teacher.

I hated that. It made me feel old. And that made me feel lonely.

Maybe it was the way the stars were aligned, maybe it was the lack of sex. I had no clue what my real problem was, but I was in a bad fucking mood when I got home.

The drinks I'd had while working the bar didn't even come close to hitting the spot, so the first thing I did when I walked in the door was pull the Stoli out of the fridge and pour myself a drink.

After kicking off my boots I carried the bottle and the glass out to the balcony and slumped into my lounge chair, still in the loose-fitting tank dress I'd worn to work. The bottle by my side and glass in my hand, I sat there in the dark and stared up at the stars, trying to make sense of the noise ripping around in my head.

It was silly to let things get to me, especially when I didn't really know what it was that was making me so pissy. But that was the nature of the darkness inside me. Sometimes I could feel it creep up and find ways to cut it off before it hit, and other times it blindsided me. I was in a good mood for the past few days, but right then all I could do was hope there was enough vodka in the bottle to make me pass out.

I downed what was still in my glass and refilled it.

Dee hadn't called back. I'd also tried to get ahold of Randy earlier, hoping to get him for the night, but he'd been at a gig out of town again. The thought of picking a random guy from the crowd and getting him to bend me over in the back alley had been there too, but my heart wasn't in it. I needed a bigger release than what I'd get like that.

A stranger would just be another Dave, and my need was beyond the itch he'd barely scratched.

Deep down I knew that I used sex to cover up how alone I felt, and when that didn't work, I buried everything I felt with alcohol. It always worked, at least for a while.

I went to take a drink and realized my glass was empty, again. The phone rang as I poured myself another drink, and I didn't even flinch.

The only person calling me at four in the morning would be Harlan. I closed my eyes and let it ring, knowing that he might be able to see me out there on the balcony, but not caring. I wasn't in the mood to talk. He'd want to know what was wrong, and I wouldn't be able to explain it to him.

The phone stopped ringing, and I wondered if maybe I should've answered it. No, it was good that I hadn't. Harlan felt like the start of something, and answering it when I was in this mood would've just ended that something before it could really start.

Before I could second-guess myself anymore, the buzzer for the building's front door screeched through my apartment. My eyes snapped open and I stood quickly, leaning over the balcony rail to see Harlan standing at the front door.

22

He was an idiot.

If she'd wanted his company she would've answered the phone. His brain knew that, yet Harlan had been unable to not head over to Kelsey's place when he'd seen her sitting on her balcony looking so alone with only her bottle for company.

She'd worn that lost look before and he'd wanted to go to her then, but he hadn't. He'd been a stranger watching her in a private moment. But he knew her now, and he wasn't going to sit by and watch while she was hurting. Not when he could help her.

Impatient, he pushed the buzzer for her apartment again, eyeing the security lock on the main door and wondering if he could pick it. The door finally clicked, unlocking loudly in the silence of the early morning. He jerked it open and took the stairs two at a time to the second floor where Kelsey waited just inside her open door. He didn't say anything, just passed by her and entered the apartment.

They stood there in the entrance hallway, silently looking at each other for a moment as the tension built. She looked beautiful. Long silky hair, curvy body made to cushion a man, and an untamed wildness in her hunter green eyes that knocked the breath right out of him.

Breaking their gaze, she drained the last of her drink and finally spoke. "What?"

"Bad night?"

She shrugged, still trying to hide from him, and probably herself too. "Would you like a drink?"

"No," he said, catching her wrist as she tried to get past. "And I don't think you need another one either."

She glared up at him, her lips twisting in a near sneer. "Yeah? What do *you* think I need?"

She'd asked him that once before, and he'd answered from the heart. This time words weren't going to do it.

"You need me," he said, then lowered his head and covered her mouth with his.

She tried to pull back, but he was having none of it. Stepping forward, he pinned her to the wall with his body and thrust his tongue between her lips roughly—claiming her as his, showing her he could give her what she needed.

Kelsey was a deeply sexual creature and she used it not only to hide behind when she felt vulnerable, but as a release when needed. He'd seen it. He could also see she needed a big release right then, and gentle coddling wasn't going to give it to her.

The empty glass fell from her hand as she tried to wiggle away, but he grabbed her other wrist and pinned them both to the wall above her head. Her gasp sent heat ripping through him and he shoved a leg between her thighs, giving her something to squirm against.

She nipped at him with sharp little teeth and he scraped his across her jawline in return. Breathy moans filled his ears as he nibbled down the bare skin of her neck to bite the muscle just above her shoulder. She moaned and her hips jerked.

One of her legs lifted and wrapped around his waist, pulling him closer as she tugged at his grip on her wrists.

She needed more.

Covering her mouth once again, he trapped both of her wrists in one hand and used the other to pull her dress up. Shoving her panties aside he thrust a finger into her wetness and started to fuck her.

She thrashed against him, twisting her head away and moaning as her hips rocked in time with his movements. Her moans turned to whimpers, not quite words, but almost pleading.

"What was that?" he asked. "Tell me what you need, Kelsey."

She moaned and kicked her heels against the back of his legs, but her hips only thrust harder against his hand.

"C'mon, Kelsey. Tell me, baby. Tell me what you need and I'll give it to you. Anything."

"More," she growled. "Give me more, damn it!"

He added another finger and bit the curve of her breast through her dress. Blood pounded through him, heating everything inside to the point where his own control was threatened. But he wouldn't lose it. She needed him, she needed this. She needed to feel safe losing control with him.

He thrust his fingers in deeper, rougher, the heel of his hand rubbing her jewelry against her clit. "Let go, Kelsey," he growled into her ear. "Let go and trust me."

She pulled and tugged at her wrists and he let go, pinning her to the wall with the weight of his body as she pushed at his shoulders, wrapping her legs around his hips at the same time. She pulled him closer then pushed against him as her cunt clenched around his fingers and she came.

Kelsey continued to move against him restlessly, ducking her head and avoiding his gaze. He pulled his hand from under her dress and lifted it to cup her chin.

"No," she whispered.

"Yes," he said. He forced her head back until he could see her face. But her eyes were closed. "Open your eyes, Kelsey. See me, the way I see you."

Chest tight, he waited for her.

Slowly, her lids lifted until they were staring at each other. Seeing each other. "That's my girl," he murmured. "I don't like it when you hide from me."

Her lips parted, and she breathed deeply, but she remained silent. Harlan could still see the wildness in her, and he could see she was fighting it.

Releasing her chin he tamped down his own desire and took a step back. He trailed his fingers over her parted lips, knowing she'd smell herself on him. When her tongue snuck out and licked at the digit, heat shot to his dick and he groaned.

"Don't ever be scared of me, Kelsey. And don't be shy. I can see all of you and I welcome every dark, dirty, and greedy part." He smiled. "And I can match them."

I looked into his blue eyes, bright with flames of desire and a barely leashed wildness that called to me like nothing else could.

"Fuck me," I begged.

My words cut the invisible leash holding him back and he snapped forward. Grabbing me around the waist, he picked me up and strode into my bedroom. He tossed me on the bed and stood at the end. "Lose the dress," he commanded.

I'd just pulled it over my head when strong hands gripped my ankles and pulled, dragging me across the bed until my ass was at the edge.

Bracing my feet against his shoulders, he reached for my lace thong and ripped it off me with one swift jerk. "Are you sure you're ready, naughty girl?" he growled.

My pussy gushed at his roughness. "Oh, yes."

He pulled a foil package from his pocket and shoved his jeans down on his hips just enough to expose the rock-hard erection bouncing against his belly. Unable to not stoke the fire in his eyes, I reached between my legs and fingered my clit while he made quick work of rolling on the condom.

Rough hands grabbed my hips and before I could suck in a breath, he'd shoved his cock deep inside me. I yelped at the sudden bite of pain mixed with the pleasure of being so full and arched off the bed.

Harlan stilled, staring down at me from his standing position. "Okay?"

I wiggled, braced my feet against his heaving chest firmly. "Oh yeah. Go hard, baby."

A grin spread across his dark features and he started to pump his hips. The angle, his size, and the heat of his stare fired me up and within seconds I was climbing toward orgasm and moaning like a porn star. I couldn't help myself, he felt too damn good.

My insides clenched, holding on to his cock with every thrust and trying to keep it in. Harlan's grip on my hips tightened and he picked up speed, pumping his hips and hitting me deep. Everything in me centered on my sex, tightening until I hit the peak and my cries filled the room.

Harlan pulled out, and before I could catch my breath he flipped me over like a rag doll, pulled my hips up until I was on my knees and thrust back into me from behind. I sighed, resting my forehead against the cool bedsheets. I could feel the darkness inside me being released and chased away with every orgasm.

"Get up," he ordered.

Hands reached under my rib cage and lifted until I was on all fours, not just ass in the air. Then those hands cupped my swinging breasts and a small moan rose within me. He found my nipples and tugged at them, sending sensations rocketing back to my core. I tossed my hair and arched my back, thrusting my breasts into his hands and my hips back against his and came again.

Harlan growled but didn't let up and the slap of skin against skin blended with my panting.

"More?"

"Yes!" I didn't want it to ever end. Sweat slicked my skin and my fingers dug into the bed as I spread my knees wider and braced myself. "Harder."

"Christ," Harlan panted. "You're fucking glorious."

He grabbed my hips, and slammed into me one . . . two . . . three times and my cunt spasmed as so much pleasure washed over me that I collapsed, limp on the bed. Harlan came down on top of me, his still clothed body blanketing mine as his chin rested against my shoulder and his panting breath warmed my cheek.

After a few moments, he kissed my cheek and pulled away gently. A small moan of disappointment escaped when I felt him withdraw, but I didn't move. I just listened quietly to the rustling sounds of him leaving my room, the toilet flushing, the tap running and then he was back.

He lifted me in his arms and I fought to open my eyes. "Hello," I whispered.

"Hello," he replied.

Then he laid me back down in the middle of the bed, stripped off his clothes, and climbed in next to me. He covered us both with a single sheet and then wrapped his arms around me, snuggling close.

I closed my eyes and breathed, deep and easy. The thought of kicking him out never even entered my mind.

He held her as she dozed. His arms wrapped around her, her body curled into his. It wasn't long before his cock hardened, swelling against the warm nest of her backside.

Still asleep, Kelsey wiggled back against him, her needy whimper drifting softly through the quiet room.

Harlan shifted, his balls growing heavy as he ran his hands over the soft woman in front of him. One hand went up to cup a full breast and tweak her nipple. Teasing and tugging on the hoop there while his other hand skimmed over smooth belly to the wet heat between her thighs.

"Yes," she whispered, rolling onto her back and parting her legs for him. "Again."

Desire punched him in the gut.

Without hesitation he stretched out on top of her. She was all soft and warm and needy beneath him, her legs parting automatically and wrapping around his waist. His belly pressing against her sex, the wetness there making his cock throb as he lowered his head and took the tip of her breast in his mouth. His tongue flicked at the hoop and he suckled.

"More," she whispered, arching her back into the caress.

She slipped a hand between them and reached for his cock. She squeezed him tight and he gasped, swelling even more in her grip. She gave him a few tugs, her hand twisting on the downward stroke in a way that sucked all the oxygen out of his brain and made him growl with pleasure.

"Slow down, sugar, or I won't last."

"No," she whimpered. "I need it now. Fuck me now."

Caught up in her urgency, he reached down and grabbed a condom from his jeans pocket. "Whatever you say."

He rolled off her and opened the foil package only to have her take the condom from his hands. Thank Christ she didn't tease him. She slid the condom on smoothly before cupping his balls and giving them a squeeze and a tug that made his cock jerk.

She grabbed his shoulders and pulled as she rolled, bringing him back on top of her. Her legs once again gripped his hips and her hand guided him to her slippery sex.

There was no style or finesse involved. He raised up on his elbows and thrust home.

"Deeper," she urged, lifting her legs and grabbing her knees, opening herself up more and he slid in to the hilt. "Harder."

Pulling back, he pumped his hips and his cock slammed in and out of her. He lifted his head and their eyes met as his balls slapped against her ass. Her beautiful eyes, so full of hunger and lust and fire that made him want to be all she wanted. All she needed.

"More!" she cried out, tossing her head back on the pillow, her body straining against his. "More, Harlan. Give me more!"

Tears formed in her eyes, and his heart pounded. Sweat slicked their skin as his hips pistoned, and he fucked her harder and deeper than he ever thought possible. And still she cried for more.

Balls tight, he was ready to explode, but there was no way he was going to go before she did. Leaning down he lowered his head and bit down on her nipple. Her hips bucked and she cried out, her cunt squeezing him and drenching him in cream at the same time.

He grunted, and thrust as deep as possible, sensation screaming through him. He gave her everything he had as his body shuddered, ecstasy exploding inside him and filling him until even his fingertips were numb.

When he could breathe again, Harlan rolled off and gathered her close. Pretending not to notice the silent tears that leaked from beneath Kelsey's closed eyes, he cuddled her close until she fell asleep.

23

On Saturday morning I woke up alone, and was relieved for it.

After stretching once, I rolled over, buried my face in my pillow, and dozed. An hour later I awoke again, and lay there staring at my ceiling, my mind racing. I just wanted to lie in bed and do nothing all day until it was time to go to work. I wanted to enjoy the truly languorous feel of my body, but I couldn't forget why I felt that way.

Even the week in Jamaica with nothing but beach, bodies, and drinks hadn't hit me the way the night with Harlan had. I'd woken up sometime during the night and turned in his arms, seeking him out, climbing on top of him and slipping his hard cock between my thighs again.

That time hadn't been fast and furious, but slow and

sensuous. Almost dreamy. And after coming again, I'd cuddled on his chest and drifted right back to sleep.

It was scary to think how well matched we were. How Harlan had been able to give me what I needed, without me even really knowing what that was. I'd been blindsided by the dark mood as I left the bar and had hated it.

I hated that I didn't understand where it came from, or why I was such a moody creature. I loved life. I'd seen and done so many things and I truly would rather be alone than in an unhappy or unhealthy relationship. I enjoyed being a bartender and being there to help others have a good time. So why was I so damn miserable at times?

The flashes in time when I felt so self-destructive scared me. I didn't understand how I could feel that way when, generally, I was happy with the life I had.

Drinking and fucking were the only things that curbed those urges inside me, but they were a temporary fix. Even I knew that. Yet, that darkness that was always below the surface of my psyche was completely gone that morning.

Climbing from bed I made my way to the shower, debating what the next step with Harlan would be. Was it just a one-night thing? It was already beyond that really.

A shiver danced through me and goose bumps raised up on my skin, despite the hot water beating down on me. Harlan seemed to know me, to accept me as I was. He appeared to be all that I'd ever wanted in a man, and that was the scariest thing of all.

* * *

Unable to spend all day doing nothing, I sat at the kitchen table with a pen and notepad, brainstorming ideas for Ariel's party.

Erotic Carnival was the theme, and all carnivals had talent, games, and rides. The talent like those guys who guessed your age or weight—so *not* something that would be enjoyed at an all-female party. The psychic Lena hired would be the talent. That left me to figure out a game, and a ride.

The temperature rose as the sun climbed higher in the sky but I didn't go out on the balcony. I couldn't.

When the phone rang and I saw Harlan's number on the caller ID, I ignored it. But the second it stopped ringing, I picked it up and dialed Dee's number from memory. There was no answer so I left another message asking her to give me a call.

Shoving everything else aside mentally, I went back to trying to figure out what to use as the *ride*.

An hour later there was a knock on my door.

Heart pounding, trepidation building, I opened the door, and let out a soft sigh of relief when I saw it wasn't Harlan on the other side.

"Hi, I'm Max Green," the five-foot-ten bald guy said as he held out his hand.

Max Green. I knew that name, but my brain wasn't beyond the fact that it wasn't Harlan yet.

He smiled softly. "The new building manager."

"Oh! Yes, I was told to expect you. I'm sorry, I'm a bit distracted. Come on in."

Max came in and sat at the kitchen table while I made some

tea. He was going to be moving in that weekend, and I was happy to hand over the keys to everything. Part of me had been hoping for a young stud that walked around in jeans and a tool belt, and nothing else, but Max Green was a sixty-one-year-old retiree with a comb-over.

He'd worked in the construction industry his whole life and the chance to stay busy with the building was exactly what he'd been looking for. "And the deal on rent helps out too," he added with a shy smile.

My fantasy man he wasn't, but I had no doubt he'd keep the building in tip-top shape. "From what I've seen in the last six weeks there's nothing big that needs to be done, but lots of little things." I told him what I'd done with Manny's sink and he promised to take another look at it first thing.

"And when the weather starts to get cold the pipes need to be bled or the units don't warm up."

Max nodded, his sharp eyes watching me carefully. "So young lady, your boyfriend giving you trouble?"

I bit back the sharp retort that popped into my head, and smiled. "I don't have a boyfriend, Max. I'm single and I live alone."

He nodded thoughtfully. "I'm sorry, I just got the impression you were expecting a different man at the door when I got here, and you seem a bit preoccupied."

"No worries," I told him. "You did surprise me, but that's not a bad thing."

Something in my face made him hesitate, but then he reached out and patted my hand as he stood. "I've learned that people come and go in our lives as we need them. We have to trust in this."

His words surprised me, but they held a ring of truth that struck a chord deep within me. I don't know what had made him say them, but they were definitely what I'd needed to hear.

"Thank you," I said as I walked him to the door. "And if you have any more questions about the building or the residents, please feel free to knock on my door anytime."

"Thank you for the tea, Kelsey. You remind me a lot of my niece. I'm sorry if I offended you by speaking too freely."

I smiled. "No offense taken. Welcome to the building, Max."

He offered me a small salute and I watched him walk down the short hallway before closing the door.

24

They're amazing, Harlan," Rick Benton said. "Top-notch."

Harlan nodded, but didn't say anything. He leaned against the wall and watched as his agent looked over his latest works. He knew they were good. With Kelsey as his muse, they could be nothing else.

"I was getting worried that you were going to be a one-shot wonder when it took you so long to get this collection together." Rick shot him an appreciative look. "But the wait was worth it. These are unique, sexy, raw, and beautiful. Completely different than your collection of blue-collar workers, yet they still have the same attention to detail and humanity. They're going to make you famous, buddy."

Pleasure washed over him. It was a very unique feeling when someone praised his art. Sort of like being in grade school and getting a gold star from your favorite teacher . . . multiplied by a hundred. "Thank you."

Rick nodded, his gaze straying back to the paintings lined up along the wall once again. "I'll start setting up some viewings this week."

"Not yet," Harlan said.

"What do you mean 'not yet'?"

Harlan appraised Rick's aggressive stance and pushed off from the wall. His agent was good at his job, but that didn't mean he could push Harlan around.

Normally Rick's attitude didn't bother him, but it was getting late in the morning and Kelsey would be awake soon. He'd have stood Rick up and stayed with her if he didn't think it would freak her out, but he knew she'd need time to think. A woman who always kicked her lovers out before they even made it to the bed would not welcome waking up to one of them still there in the morning.

Even if they both new something special was happening between them.

The urge to check on her and ensure that she wasn't going to pretend that nothing had happened between them was strong, but first, he had to deal with Rick.

He sighed. "I'm letting you see them so you'll get off my back, but I'm not ready to show them to anyone else yet."

"I know you'll need to do a few more pieces for a full showing, at least two, maybe even three." Rick frowned. "But what you have here is enough for me to show around and create a buzz.

We want this next show to be even bigger than the first one, which means plenty of advance publicity."

"Not yet."

"Why not?"

"Because I said so."

Rick shook his head. "Not good enough, buddy."

Christ, he was a pushy bastard.

That's what happened when one let a friend become an advisor. Although he had to admit, if it hadn't been for Rick's aggressive persistence, Harlan wouldn't have even pursued painting as a career. Then he'd never have sold out of his first collection, or bought the loft and moved here, which meant he might never have met Kelsey.

"I need to show these to someone before we can shop them around."

Comprehension dawned on Rick's face and he turned back to the painting in front of him. It was of a naked woman, straddling a wooden chair backward with her back arched, dark hair streaming down her back. The woman was done in loving detail, down to the ripe berry color of her nipples, while the chair beneath her was almost part of the background. There was nothing shocking or out there about the image, but the expression on the beauty's face said it all. Rick examined it more closely, and Harlan waited.

"If she doesn't like them what are you going to do?" Rick faced him, his hands slicing through the air as he spoke passionately. "You have so much talent, Harlan. You can be one of the greats, but art is also a business, and if we don't get you out there again soon your career could be over before it really starts."

Harlan's gut clenched. He wasn't really worried about his "career." He loved working for himself, but not showing or being able to support himself with his art didn't make him any less an artist. It wouldn't take away his love of painting, or the freedom to let his imagination take form on the canvas. He'd always be an artist. And if he had to go back to work to make ends meet, then he would. Jobs were never hard to find for an ironworker with his experience and skills.

What did worry him, just a little, was Kelsey's reaction when she saw the collection she'd inspired. And he knew he couldn't show her the whole collection yet. She just wasn't ready to see herself the way he saw her.

"Give me another couple of weeks, and I'll have a full collection for you."

"A full one?"

"It might not be all of these exact ones." He waved at the paintings behind him. "But yes, a full collection."

By the time Rick left the loft it was almost three o'clock. Harlan picked up the phone and called Kelsey, but there was no answer. Either she wasn't home, or she saw his number on the caller ID and was ignoring him. Either way, he decided not to push it. He had two weeks to plan a complete collection.

25

The nightclub was open, but empty, and I was just about done setting up the bar when Samair came down the stairs from Val's office. Instead of going through the back and heading home, she stopped at the end of the bar.

"Woo hooo!" she hooted. "Someone got lucky."

I grinned and didn't bother to deny it. "Can I get you a drink?"

"Tequila and seven, please." She practically bounced on her toes as I poured her drink. "Well, aren't you going to share the details?"

Some people might be offended by that question coming from someone who would usually be classified only as a casual friend. But Samair wasn't being facetious, and I needed to tell someone what was going on since Dee still hadn't called me back. So, I spilled the whole story to her as other staff members wandered into the club to start their shifts.

"So you met this guy because he was spying on you?"

"Yeah, sort of." I rushed to wipe the skeptical look from her face. "I know it sounds creepy, but it wasn't. There were times when I felt like someone might be watching me, but I dismissed it as my imagination. Then when I did catch sight of him, I realized, first, that I was relieved I wasn't going crazy. And second, the whole vibe wasn't creepy. It was a bit of a turn-on actually."

"So you're not worried he's a psycho stalker?"

"No. He's an artist."

Samair waved her hand blithely. "Same thing."

We laughed and I shook my head. "No, it makes a weird sort of sense because most artists are slightly reclusive, and people watchers at the same time. Right?"

And like Max had said, people come and go in life as you need them. I might've forgotten it, but I did believe that. Too many odd coincidences had led me to where I was in life to not believe it.

Meeting Jesse in Dublin had been wonderful. He'd shown me that I was capable of feeling more than sexual attraction for a man. I obviously hadn't been ready for more than that then, but it was nice to know I was capable of it.

Val had certainly entered my life at a time I needed him. I'd given up hope of ever finding a place where I fit, a place where I could be loud and flirtatious and cocky and confident and be praised for it. Risqué had become a second home to me, and that I didn't always feel that way anymore was heartbreaking.

And it hit me. The darkness hadn't blindsided me the night before. I'd just managed to ignore the way it had been creeping in on me lately because I hadn't wanted to admit how alone I'd truly felt. But the night before, when I'd had nothing better to do on a Friday night than cover a shift for another bartender, I'd watched all the shit that went on in the club, and felt left out.

I was there, I was a key part of Val's staff, but I was older than the others, and that made me different to them. I could joke and laugh and flirt with them all, and it went both ways, but I wasn't *part* of them. I didn't belong anymore.

I remembered all the times they planned birthday outings, or get-togethers after work in front of me, but never invited me to join in. Fuck, I'd probably have said no, but it would've been nice to be asked. It was stupid. To be hurt or feel left out by people I didn't even really want to hang out with.

But as I watched Samair sip her drink and nod hello to DJ Rob, I acknowledged it wasn't so much the staff at Risqué . . . it was everyone.

It was knowing that when Dee and I got together it was because *I called her.* It was knowing that my mother bragged about my cousin's baby to her friends instead of her daughter's good work ethic or world travels. It was the fact that my younger, more conservative sister was getting married while I wondered if I was even capable of finding acceptance for all of me.

Independence and strength were instilled in me from birth, and I valued them. I *liked* being able to take care of myself. But that didn't mean I always wanted to, and deep down, I couldn't help but think that made me weak. And that made me angry.

Samair took a sip from her drink and smiled at me. "So, what's his name?"

"Harlan Shaw." I remembered the fingerprint bruises on my hips and the teeth marks on my shoulder this morning. Harlan had taken care of me but good, and he hadn't made me feel weak at all.

"Have you seen any of his artwork? Been to his place? What else do you know about him?"

I rolled my eyes. "C'mon Samair, since when am I not a good judge of character? Besides that, I like things a little freaky from time to time."

That might've been an understatement, but it was one I could live with. It was better than saying, "Sometimes I crave a bit of pain and he knows just how to give it to me."

I took a sip from my own drink and pinned Samair with my gaze. "Besides, you can't tell me that you and Val don't get more adventurous than most . . . I've caught you a time or two. Remember?"

The pretty blonde blushed, but she couldn't hide the smile that crept across her lips. "Val is definitely not what I'd call traditional."

"And aren't you glad for it?"

She nodded and we both laughed. "See, unconventional is not always bad."

"One could never mistake you for conventional, Kelsey," Samair said and waved her hand at my black latex bra, fishnet shirt, and short mini. "Speaking of conventional, Ariel was in for a fitting today."

We talked about Ariel's dress, and my plans for the party, until Joey arrived and joined Samair at the bar. The two women had known each other for years and were super close, but I wasn't excluded from the conversation at all.

Just the opposite, in fact. And when talk turned to sex once more, as the three of us graded the guys that walked around the club like they were modeling just for us, I decided it was time I made more of an effort to find some real friends. Friends like them.

The night went by super fast, and I was full of positive energy when I got home. As I parked my car in the back lot I wished I could just go over to Harlan's. You'd think getting fucked so much in the last twenty-four hours would make me want to sleep, but it didn't.

I wanted more. But not just more sex, more Harlan.

With a drink in one hand and a book I couldn't get into in the other, it occurred to me that he was fast becoming an addiction.

The phone rang just after 4:00 a.m. and I smiled.

Just roll with it, Kelsey, I told myself. *Be casual, and let things happen.*

It was a bit weird, to sit on my balcony in the dark, and look at the stars and talk to a man I barely knew. Yet, we did know each other. We might not have had a traditional start, but that was probably a good thing. Traditional wasn't my strong suit.

Besides, having him be someone who didn't know Kelsey the bartender, or Kelsey the sister, or even Kelsey the friend, was just as freeing as meeting strangers in foreign countries.

He knew the real me. No, that's not it. I'm always real, I just don't always show all of myself to people. With Harlan, I felt like I didn't have to hide any of myself. To him I was the naughty girl next door, and that was it.

Which was just what I wanted.

When the sun started to peek over the horizon I groaned. "I shouldn't even go to bed, I should just stay up and get myself to the freakin' mall as soon as it opens."

"The mall?" His rusty chuckle echoed over the phone line, warming me. "Somehow I never figured you for a shopping queen."

I mentioned my frustration at finding a present for my sister and he suggested some art. "You said you love art, and that they're not living together yet, right?"

"Yeah."

"So, she's going to want to bring something new into the house with her when she moves in. It doesn't matter how nice his place is, she'll want something that is new, and hers. Or *theirs*, and not just his."

I laughed. "Sort of like marking her territory, huh?"

"Exactly."

Strangely, I could totally see Ariel feeling that way. "It's a great idea. Thank you."

"I know just the place you should shop at. What do you say you head to bed and catch a few hours' sleep and I'll pick you up at noon?"

"Hmmm." I thought about it. I was still full of energy. "I think the better plan would be to go have some breakfast, fuel up, and hit the stores before they get busy."

"You need to get some sleep. You just don't know it."

"Shit, I'm ready now."

"Yeah?" He laughed. "Well *I* need a shower and a nap, so I'll see you in a couple of hours."

He hung up and I had to shake off the urge to go climb into the shower with him.

26

Harlan showed up at my door and I was ready to go, dressed in a frayed denim miniskirt, a black T-shirt, and black biker boots that laced all the way up my calves. I'd let my hair hang long and straight down my back and my only makeup was mascara and some harlot red lipstick.

A cross between Betty Boop and Bettie Page, I was feeling sexy and confident. And the appreciation in Harlan's eyes when I opened the door told me I looked *good*.

His lips tilted up in one corner when he saw the small silver handcuff decal in the center of my chest, but he didn't say anything. So I didn't bother to show him the back. He'd see it soon enough.

"Ready?" he asked.

"Definitely," I said as I closed up my apartment. "If I don't find a gift today I'm going to get them the eighty-dollar toaster."

"We'll find them something. Tell me about your sister and her fiancé."

There was a cab waiting in front of the apartment and Harlan directed me to it with a firm hand at the small of my back.

"I can drive us," I said as we got closer to it. "We don't need to take a cab."

"Parking on a Sunday is going to be a pain in the ass. Let's stick with the cab."

He held open the back door, and slid in after me, directing the cabbie to Granville Island. I almost smacked myself in the forehead. An old abandoned industrial park near downtown that had been renovated and remade into a commercial park and artist community—it was full of galleries, workshops, pubs, and restaurants.

Better than any mall, Granville Island was the perfect place to look for a unique, one-of-a-kind gift.

After directing the cabby, Harlan leaned back in the seat, close enough that his leg rubbed against mine, and I grinned.

"Oh, now I see the real benefits to a cab," I said and laid my hand on his thigh. Hard muscle flexed beneath my hand and my hormones did a little dance.

Harlan covered my hand with his and winked. "Tell me about your sister and her fiancé," he said again.

If he hadn't kept my hand on his thigh, I would've felt rebuffed, but the gleam in his eye and the way his hand tightened on mine said he was just as aware of the physical possibilities as I was.

I batted my eyelashes and told him about Ariel and Miles.

"Ariel's the complete opposite of me. Even though she's the younger sister, she's definitely the more responsible of the two of us. She was a straight A student, went to college right out of high school and got her accountants certification, or whatever it is, and has been doing the same work ever since. She works for herself, which is how she met Miles. She's the bookkeeper for his bookstore. Their wedding date is a year to the day of their first date. That draw a good picture?"

"Your apartment building went condo right?"

Huh? "Yeah, the owner sold off half of the units a few years ago. The other half he and his partner still own, and rent out, but it's run as a condo with a board and all that. Why?"

"You own yours, right?"

"Yes."

"And you work a full-time job and pay your own way?"

Confusion reigned. "Yes, what are you getting at?"

He turned his head, his blue eyes pinning me to the spot. "Then I don't want to hear you imply that your sister, or anyone else, is better or more responsible than you simply because they are more straitlaced. You own your home, pay your own way, and do your own thing. That's not something everyone can say."

Stunned, I stared at him.

He leaned close and spoke clearly. "And I really like the way you do your own thing."

His lips pressed down on mine and fireworks sparked deep inside me. I turned toward him, curled my hands into his shirt, and tried to pull him closer only to have him pull back.

"Such an enchantingly eager girl you are." His blue eyes

gleamed and his hand ran up my bare thigh, leaving a trail of fire in its wake. "You don't have to work tonight, do you?"

Unable to force words past the lump of desire lodged in my throat, I simply shook my head.

"That's why you needed to sleep this morning, because I'm not going to give you any rest tonight."

Once there, Harlan acted as guide. A very mellow and easy-going type of guide, but there was no doubt he knew what he was talking about, or that he was in charge.

We were dropped off at one end of Railspur Alley and we walked the whole street, going in and out of almost every gallery and store. He pointed out different items to me, using anything as an excuse to brush against me. The constant rub of his body against mine, his hand against my ass, his arm across my chest, his breath feathering across my cheek as he explained something—it was a slow, sensual torture that had my sex throbbing and my mind going completely blank.

When we walked into the ceramics store I found way too many things I wanted for myself. Yet, nothing I thought Ariel would connect with.

"Do you have something for sale in any of these stores?" I asked.

He shook his head. "Not right now, no. I had an exhibit up six months ago, and my agent's trying to get another one up soon, but I haven't finished the collection I'm working on yet."

"Collection?"

"Since I don't have a gallery of my own or rent space in one, I freelance. I'll do a show with a full collection of themed work, and if it doesn't sell in that time then we'll shop the pieces around to galleries as individuals."

"Hmm." It made sense. Sort of. I didn't really care how it all worked. I just wondered when I'd get to see some of his stuff.

As if reading my mind he nudged me toward a different display. "If you're a good girl, I'll show you what I'm working on later."

"Yeah?"

"Yeah."

"A *good* girl?" I asked, arching an eyebrow at him.

He laughed and bumped against me playfully. "*My* definition of good isn't what you would call typical."

"Are you going to share your definition with me?"

The corner of his mouth lifted and his eyes gleamed, but he remained silent as we walked through the big artists co-op building.

A few minutes later he led me to the back corner display.

"As much as I'd love for you to get an oil painting for them, because I think everyone should buy oil paintings," he said, "from what you've said about your sister and her fiancé, I think a sculpture would be something they'd enjoy more. Something like this maybe?"

"Ohh," I said. It was all I could say. There were half a dozen pieces in the display, and each one was beautiful and functional.

Bowls of all sizes, all in shimmering multicolored glass. The colors blended, swirling and sparkling together in a way that made them almost seem alive. "These are perfect."

A salesman came over and spoke to Harlan while I examined the bowls. They were exactly something Ariel would love. Pretty, and useful. She could put it in the entranceway as a place to drop keys and mail, or in the center of a dining table. Even empty the bowl itself was enough to draw attention.

It occurred to me that Miles might not like them, but then, from what I knew of Miles, if Ariel loved it, he'd let her put it anywhere she wanted.

Now, to decide on only one.

Glancing at the price made that choice easier. I picked a medium-sized one with green and gold over a black base and showed it to Harlan. "This one."

When Harlan tried to pay I glared at him so hard I'm sure he felt flames lick at his skin. I did let him arrange to have the bowl delivered to my place though.

"What now?" I asked when we exited the store.

"One store in particular I want to stop in, then we can do whatever you want." He wrapped my hand in his and led me to a shop. When we entered and I saw colorful silks everywhere, I was a little surprised. I'd expected something more . . . manly.

Harlan walked slowly and I trailed after him, reaching out to touch every now and then. Pillows, clothing, bags and bolts . . . everything was silk.

We reached a small display of scarves and Harlan pulled one

out. It was black with shots of deep purple and blue woven throughout. He lifted my hand and wrapped it around my wrist. "How does it feel?" he asked.

Instant heat flooded my system. A silk scarf was wrapped around my wrist and Harlan's hard chest was pressing against my back.

"Feel good, greedy girl?" he whispered, his lips brushing against my ear.

I nodded. "Oh, yeah."

Harlan brushed my hair aside and placed his hand between my shoulder blades. "Did you think I wouldn't notice what's on the back of your T-shirt?"

"I hoped you would." My words sounded breathy and barely there, even to me. While I'd never been restrained in sex play before, it had always been a fantasy of mine, and the T-shirt clearly stated it with the words "Cuff Me, Fuck Me" written across the back.

Harlan chuckled and stepped back, taking the scarf with him. "Pick out a few then, sweetheart. I want half a dozen."

My mind swam with ways to use half a dozen silk scarves in sex play, and there was no doubt whatsoever that these were going to be for sex play. Not when the fire in his eyes matched the one in my belly.

We left the shop and started toward the entrance to Granville Island to find a cab. Butterflies had suddenly given birth in my stomach and I searched for something to distract myself.

"So, what's next?" I finally asked, trying not to stare at the bag Harlan now carried.

His lips twitched and he glanced down at me. "It's still early, and I haven't been to the seawall yet this summer. Will you walk it with me?"

"Sure. That sounds nice."

As nice as it sounded, it wasn't what I really wanted to do, but what was I going to say—"No, I want to take you home and fuck you?"

It wasn't far to Stanley Park, where the five-mile seawall traveled the edge of the park, but we caught a taxi anyway.

Once we settled in the backseat Harlan's hand crept up my thigh. "Are you wearing underwear, Kelsey?"

Butterflies batted against my stomach and I nodded. "A thong."

"Take it off."

Excitement zinged through me and my nipples throbbed. "Why don't you take it off for me?" I asked.

His eyes narrowed but he rose to the challenge. Not bothering to try and be subtle or hide what he was doing from the driver, he reached across my lap, slid both hands under my skirt and grabbed the elastic resting on my hips. "Lift," he commanded.

I lifted and he pulled, skimming them right down my legs and off.

I'd been hoping for a quick nudge or tickle while his hands were under there, but no such luck. "You really get off on torturing me, don't you?"

"You have no idea what torture is like." One side of his mouth lifted in a half smile. "But you will."

Heat crept up my neck and flooded my cheeks when he lifted my damp panties to his face and inhaled.

Harlan didn't say anything; he just put the panties away in the bag with the silk scarves, and then reached for my hand again. Only this time he didn't put it on his thigh. He brought it over his lap and put it directly on his zipper.

The hardness there burned against my hand and I'd just started to play with the zipper tab when the taxi pulled into the park. It was a warm and bright Sunday, and the place was packed with walkers, bikers, and tourists taking pictures of . . . everything.

We got out and walked along for a bit, gazing out at the ocean, not talking, just holding hands like teenagers. The butterflies disappeared, my arousal lowering to a steady hum, kept lightly on edge because I had no panties on.

We walked, the sun warm on my face, and a strange peacefulness came over me. There was no pressure to talk, to question or converse. No hunger to do more than we were doing.

Never had I felt so comfortable with another person. Not even Dee or Ariel.

Not far along the seawall Harlan veered off the track to follow one of the forest trails.

"Harlan?"

"What?" he glanced at me. "You scared to go to a less public place with me?"

The question was said with humor, but the gleam in his eyes promised a seriously good time. Adrenaline roared front and center and I was suddenly hyperaware of my bare pussy.

The trail wasn't steep, or overly hard to navigate, but the farther from the water's edge and the deeper into the forest, the fewer people we passed. And the faster Harlan walked.

He let go of my hand and moved in front of me, which I did not mind at all because the view of his denim-covered ass was much better than any flora or fauna we passed.

"C'mon, Kelsey," he urged in a silky voice when I started to fall behind.

"Harlan, as much as I'm enjoying the view of your amazing ass, I have a short skirt and leather boots on. I am not dressed for hiking a trail."

He turned to smile at me. "And no panties. I haven't forgotten that very important fact, and you shouldn't either."

Ohhhh, it was *that* kind of walk we were on.

"Promises, promises," I muttered loud enough for him to hear. But new energy filled me and I started walking again.

The trees shaded the path and Harlan confidently pointed out the different types of trees and the occasional wildflower. A cute squirrel crossed the path just in front of us and ran up a nearby tree. Just as I was getting into the images of naked frolicking in a public park that were flittering through my mind, the trail began getting rough.

Maybe because Harlan had turned off the trail and was veering into a patch of dense trees.

I was only three steps behind him, and when a tree branch

snapped back and hit me in the chest I threw up my hands. "That's it!" I cried, stumbling a little, breathless and sweaty. Not even the promise of naked frolicking was worth this.

Hands reached through the trees and gripped my arms, pulling me through and bringing me against a rock-hard chest. Holding me to his solid chest, he kissed my cheek and whispered in my ear, "Done, my girl. Now you get your reward."

His lips locked onto mine and I gave up my fight for breath. This kind of breathlessness I enjoyed. Firm hands slid down my back and gave my ass cheeks a hard squeeze.

Harlan was already hard and the feel of his throbbing cock pressing against my belly made my tired body hum with anticipation. Gripping his wide shoulders, I sagged against him and let him ravage my mouth.

Even though I wanted to fuck energetically in the sunshine, after that little jaunt through the woods, I didn't have the energy to do much more than spread my legs for him.

As if sensing this, Harlan dragged his lips across my cheek, and whispered in my ear, "Poor little horny girl. You had a hard time on the trail, didn't you?"

I nodded and tilted my head back. Taking the hint, Harlan trailed his lips across my throat. After giving my ass a final squeeze one hand slid up my body to cup a breast. My nipple hardened beneath the thin T-shirt, pouting for attention, and I whimpered in need.

He backed me up a couple of steps until I felt the solid roughness of a fallen tree against my bare calves. "I want you to sit down on this log and I'll make you forget all about the trail, and the people still on it."

God, he knew just the right thing to say to get my juices flowing. "Do people come this way?"

He gripped the hem of my skirt, and when I sat, the skirt lifted so that my bare bottom scraped on the rough bark of the fallen tree log. "Someone is going to come. Again and again, I promise."

With a wicked smile he dropped to the ground in front of me and spread my knees apart. Leaning forward, he cut off any other protest with an openmouthed kiss that caused all thoughts of discovery to flee from my mind. When he pulled back he lifted my T-shirt and pushed down the cups of my bra until my tits plumped up over the edge, nipples flushed, hard, and aching.

He lowered his mouth to one nipple and rolled the other around with thumb and forefinger. Each pinch on one was countered with a sharp bite on the other. My whimpers and gasps drowned out the nearby singing birds as sharp arrows of pleasure shot from my nipples to my core.

The hard ridge of Harlan's erection pressed against my pussy and I rubbed against him like a cat in heat. A deep groan rumbled out of him as he pulled his mouth from my tit and shifted away. Without any further foreplay he used his thumbs to spread my plump pussy lips crudely apart and placed his mouth directly on my exposed clit. A jolt shot through me, straightening my spine and spreading my legs wider.

He didn't thrust any fingers in, or even pay any attention to my entrance, he focused completely on the rigid button now poking out from its protective hood. He sucked and the ring piercing pulled roughly, he nibbled and shivers of delight danced through my body. He alternated sucking and biting until waves of pleasure crashed over me and I cried out.

When the waves dissipated I became aware that Harlan was gently lapping at the juices that flowed freely from my cunt, and the tightness deep in my belly signaled another orgasm was close. A stiff finger thrust inside my tunnel as his tongue began working my hard nub again. A second finger soon joined the first and the thrusts picked up. My hips rocked forward and my fingers tangled in his hair, clutching him firmly to me as another set of waves crashed over me.

"Feel better?" he asked when I could breathe normally again. His hands cupped my head and he placed a soft kiss on my lips.

"Uh-huh," I hummed in response, tasting myself on his lips and tongue.

"My turn now." He pulled me off the log and instructed me to bend over it, tilting my bare ass into the cool fresh air. "Look at that view, eh? Awesome." A firm hand caressed my exposed cheeks and I wondered if he was talking about his view, or mine.

My breasts scraped against the log as I positioned myself and looked at the view for the first time. It really was an impressive sight. A peaceful haven in the middle of a crowded park. I could see the ocean beyond the trees and for the first time I wondered just how far we'd gone from the actual seawall. We'd walked for a while, but the trail had been pretty twisted. I heard the cries of kids playing on the beach blend with the birds singing and wondered briefly if they could hear my cries of pleasure down at the water.

The rasp of a zipper echoed loudly in our small clearing and

I shook my ass in anticipation. Harlan growled in appreciation and I grinned. A firm hand smacked one of my cheeks sharply and I yelped.

"You have an amazing ass, girl."

I glanced over my shoulder and our eyes met and held. The pure want in his eyes sparked a flame deep inside me, in a place that had never before been touched. My heart stuttered and I tore my gaze away, instinctively wiggling my ass at him again.

Needing no further encouragement, a firm hand gripped my hip while another guided his impressive length into me. Once inside my slick tunnel he anchored both hands on my hips and immediately began a steady rhythm. With every thrust my tits swayed and brushed my sensitized nipples against the log.

"Oh fuck, yeah, fuck. That's it," I urged him on. "Harder."

Harlan thrust faster, one of his hands leaving my hips to slide up my back and grip my shoulder, bracing me. Guttural grunts and groans floated away on the breeze as the walls of my cunt clenched hungrily. I was going to come again. Soon.

Harlan was puffing like a steam engine going uphill so I braced my hands firmly on the other side of the log, arched my back, rolled my hips and felt his cock hit that sweet spot deep inside me.

"Ugh," he grunted.

His hands tightened their grip on my body and he slammed into me a final time, holding us tight together as the cock inside me swelled and throbbed hotly. The walls of my cunt clenched in answer to his orgasm and my eyes slid closed as my own ripped through my body.

I collapsed onto the log, Harlan's body covering mine. With his head resting between my shoulder blades we looked out at the trees and I figured that for sure someone had heard our cries carried away by the breeze. I hoped so anyway.

27

The walk back was a lot easier and slower after our little bush escapade. As soon as we exited the trail and were in the open, Harlan wrapped his arm around my shoulders and kept me tight to his side.

Catching a cab was no trouble, and we picked up a pizza on the way home. There was no question of the date ending when we climbed out of the cab, but Harlan surprised me by leading me to his place instead of mine.

"Oh, I get to see the artist's lair, do I?"

"If you're a good girl I might even show you some art."

"A good girl, huh?" I tilted my head and licked my lips suggestively. "I got the impression you liked the bad girl in me."

He wrapped an arm around my waist and pulled me tight against him. "I like all of you. Good girl, bad girl, greedy girl, and horny girl." He kissed me fast and hard then set me aside. He handed me the pizza box and the bag of silk scarves so he could unlock the door.

I followed him up a set of stairs and down a very dim hall.

The building wasn't new by any means, and it showed. The halls were dim and the carpet beneath our feet worn. Someone in the building was cooking curry and my stomach growled loudly.

Harlan chuckled. "Two more minutes," he said.

"It's the curry," I explained. "Even if I wasn't hungry, which I am, the scent of curry always sends my gut into a panic for food."

"A good panic? Do you like curry, or not like it?" He opened to door to his place and waved me in.

"I love curry. I spent a few months in India and became addicted."

All thoughts fled as I stared around Harlan's loft. It was amazing. Open and airy, it was half painter's studio and half industrial warehouse bedroom style. Ignoring my rumbling stomach I wandered the room. A king-sized bed was against the far wall, its rumpled sheets looking very inviting. The black iron headboard and footboard brought the silk scarves to mind and my pussy clenched.

There was a black iron clothing rack, and a big folding screen that could obviously be extended to create a wall between the bed and the rest of the room.

An overstuffed sofa and two armchairs were arranged in the middle of the room with a TV, stereo, and entertainment center set up against the wall.

"Kitchen's this way," Harlan said, reaching for my hand.

I took his hand and wondered if he'd deliberately interrupted my gazing then, just as my feet had started for the area that was obviously his workspace.

The kitchen followed the same open concept as the rest of the place. The stainless steel fridge and stove making it look all industrial and clean. Harlan set the pizza on the island and waved me to a stool. I sat and opened the box.

"I've got coffee, orange juice, beer, or water. What would you like to drink?" he asked as he pulled plates from the cupboard.

Beyond being polite or shy, I reached for the biggest piece of pepperoni pizza I could see, and started munching.

After setting a couple of glasses of juice on the counter, Harlan parked himself on the stool next to me and we ate in silence. Once the initial hunger was satisfied I picked up a second slice and glanced at him. "Why do you keep beer in the fridge if you don't drink?"

"Occasionally I have friends over who do drink."

"So it's not that you think drinking is all bad, you yourself just don't do it."

"I think social drinking is fine, even though I myself don't do it."

We were quiet for another minute, and I argued with myself about whether I was being too nosy. I didn't want to piss him off, or insult him, but I found that I *did* want to get to know him.

Finally, I gave in and opened my mouth. "Will you tell me why you don't drink?"

"Are you sure you really want to know?"

"Sure. Why wouldn't I?"

He chewed for a minute, thinking. Then he put down his pizza and met my gaze. "People think drinking makes them feel better, but in reality alcohol is a depressant. It doesn't make a person's problems or feelings go away, it only masks them for a time. And when it stops masking them, people drink more, until they become either self-destructive, or completely uncaring."

I straightened. "You think everyone who drinks is going to turn into an alcoholic?"

He shook his head. "No. But I do think some people are pre-disposed to becoming one. Like I am."

Whoa!

He must've read my thoughts on my face because a rusty chuckle escaped him and he shook his head again. "No, I'm not an alcoholic. But I do have a bit of an addictive personality. I tend to jump into everything I do, wholeheartedly, and that includes drinking, and drugs." He smiled at her. "We're alike in that way."

I didn't know what to think. I guess I should've known that asking questions like that would bring us into some serious territory, but I hadn't thought.

What was I supposed to say to his confession? Or was his confession even the point of what he said? Sure I drank a lot, but I wasn't an alcoholic. I was drinking juice instead of beer, wasn't I?

Shit. It was time to switch gears. "We're alike, huh? Does that mean you're feeling the need to get naked again too?"

Harlan threw back his head and laughed, and my spirit

lightened. Then he stood abruptly and suddenly I was upside down over his shoulder, staring at his ass.

"Such a greedy girl," he said. One arm wrapped around my legs, and a warm hand slid up the back of my thigh as he left the kitchen and moved through the loft. "It's a good thing I think I'm addicted to you."

The hand cupped my bare ass cheek and patted it lightly . . . then suddenly his hand came down a bit harder, making me gasp as cream slicked my pussy.

"You like that, don't you?" he asked.

I thought he was going for the bed, but instead, he set me down in the middle of the room, in front of the sofa. "Strip," he ordered.

Part of me wanted to challenge the order, but more of me loved the fire in his eyes and was eager to play. I got rid of my shirt in one smooth move, and then dropped my skirt. I stood there in nothing but my bra and my boots, feeling unbelievably naughty and sexy.

Harlan's eyes swept over me, causing my nipples to peak and my clit to throb.

"As much as I love to have you watch me," I said as I reached for him, "I was hoping we could *both* get naked this time."

I got his shirt off before he whipped off his belt and told me to turn around. "Knees on the edge of the sofa, hands on the back of it," he said. "There's something I've been wanting to do to you for a while."

Breath rasping in my throat, I turned and did as he asked.

"So pretty, all this white skin. It's almost a shame to mark it." He trailed the end of his belt down my back and over my buttocks teasingly. I arched my back and thrust my ass out farther, making him laugh. "I said almost."

Then he hit me.

Not with the belt, but with his hand.

More slaps were quick to follow and soon there was no denying that getting spanked turned me on more than ever before. I squirmed and sighed, arching my back, wiggling my ass, and spreading my thighs in blatant invitation to be touched. But Harlan didn't stop.

His slaps softened a bit, and then lowered so that his hand was landing on the under curve of my cheeks and his fingertips were landing on my swollen pussy lips.

"Oh yeah!" I moaned.

Then his hand was gone, and the only sound in the room was my heavy breathing. I looked over my shoulder and saw Harlan just staring at my ass. The look in his eyes was pure lust.

My heart pounded and blood rushed to my cunt. My inner muscles clenched, searching for him.

Mouth dry and throat tight with desire, I forced myself to speak. "Harlan?"

"You have an ass made for spanking, and pink is definitely your color, my girl." Harlan stepped up and ran a hand over the curve of my rump lovingly. "Let's see some more of it, shall we?"

Folding the belt in half, he went to work. First my ass, then my thighs, then one cheek, then the other, then my thigh. Pain flooded my system, blending with my arousal and making me incoherent as I floated on a sea of sensation.

My ass throbbed, my thighs throbbed, my pussy throbbed until I finally pushed against the back of the sofa and begged.

"Harlan, more. Stop. Please," I gasped. "You. I need *you*."

Then he smacked my pussy with the strap.

A tremor shook me and I cried out. He did it again and again. "Please," I cried, tears running down my cheeks.

Dropping his belt Harlan slid his hand between my thighs and slapped my pussy three times sharply, hitting me in a way that had the hard jewel on my piercing digging directly into my clit, setting off my orgasm.

I shook and shivered and moaned as sensation rocked my insides. The room tilted and once again I was in Harlan's arms. He crossed the room and set me down gently in the middle of his bed.

I gazed at him, hungry for more, and thrilled to see that same intense hunger reflected back at me.

28

Harlan laid her on the bed and sucked in a deep breath. Emotion beyond sexual arousal filled his chest and clogged his throat. Reaching down he gently removed Kelsey's bra, before stripping his own clothes off.

Still and silent in the middle of his bed, her eyes tracked all of his movements and drank in every inch of bare skin as he revealed it.

It was the first time anyone had ever watched him so closely, and he felt her gaze as if it were her hands. He wondered if that was how she felt when he watched her. If she could feel his gaze even across the street.

When he lowered himself onto the bed, next to her, Kelsey immediately reached for him, her soft sigh of pleasure music to his ears.

He'd worried, for just a moment, that he'd gone too far with his spanking. But the combination of gratitude and desire still in her darkening eyes reassured him. She was as passionate and eager as ever.

Now it was time for him to reassure her.

He covered her body with his, and kissed her. Gently, savoring her taste, her feel, he began to explore her.

He cupped her breasts and suckled at the nipples, he kissed each rib until she was gasping and arching into every caress. His fingertips skimmed over the baby smooth skin inside her elbow, and behind her knee.

Hot lava flowed through his veins, keeping him steady and sure as he loved her. When her breathy moans turned to pleas, he reached into the bedside drawer and quickly sheathed himself.

Settling between her legs he slid into her body easily, her warm wetness welcoming him, surrounding him. Braced on his elbows he stared into Kelsey's eyes and began to move.

Her hands gripped his shoulders, her thighs cradled his hips and she rocked with him. Sweat slicked their skin, and she cupped the back of his head, tugging him down until their lips were touching.

She licked his lips and nipped at the bottom one, then soothed it with a long kiss that made his balls tighten and the pressure build to bursting at the base of his cock. She pulled back slightly, gasping and wrapping her legs around his hips.

"Come for me, Harlan." Her eyes glowed as she smiled. "Please."

Unable to hold back any longer, Harlan picked up his speed

and thrust hard, his balls tightened and tingled and that was it. Every muscle in his body snapped tight and sparks went off behind his eyes as pleasure swamped his system.

Harlan came awake slowly, his hand automatically searching the bed for Kelsey, and closing on a cold piece of paper. He lay there on his back, waiting for his eyes to adjust to the light now flooding the loft before he attempted to read the note.

He'd come so hard he passed out.

He had a dim recollection of Kelsey snuggled in his arms as he slept, and of her creeping out from his arms and kissing his cheek.

He could've stopped her if he'd really wanted to, but it had been an intense night. Her cut and run reaction didn't surprise him. Her note did though.

Scrubbing a hand over his face once more he peeled his eyes open and focused.

Thank you.

Thank you for what? For the date? For the pizza? For the fuck?

Thank you for finally breaking through her shield just a little bit?

And he *was* breaking through her shield. She'd spent the day with him, more than twelve hours. When they'd not talked, the silence had been comfortable. When they had talked, it had been about real things, not just sex. Of course they'd had sex, and oh, what sex it was. She was everything he'd thought she was, and more. He didn't understand why she kept such tight control on herself. Why she worked so hard to appear tough and carefree when just below the surface, she was seething with emotion and passion.

He glanced over to the work space side of his loft and wondered if she'd checked out the paintings before she'd left. There was no doubt a couple of them would be fine with her—she did offer to pose for him—but there were two he wasn't sure she was ready to see just yet. They showed what *he* saw in her, not just the surface she worked so hard to uphold.

There was no way she'd looked at them. If she had, she would've woken him up. Shy and quiet was one thing Kelsey was not, and those particular paintings would certainly get a reaction.

29

I spent all day Monday on the phone or the Internet, lining up the goodies for Ariel's party. With less than a week to get it all together, there was no time to dick around. Plus, keeping busy with that stuff kept me from obsessing about time spent with Harlan.

Lucky for me, Lacey's contacts paid off big-time. I found privacy screens to separate the party room into sections on my third phone call. And since I only needed two screens, the short notice wasn't a big deal.

Lacey detailed her food plan, and I knew it would be a big hit. Even my mom would like it. I called Samair and asked her if she could make me something, anything small and relatively cheap, for the guest goodie bags.

"Do you want each bag to have the same item?" she asked. "Or can they be different items of the same value, that sort of thing?"

"If different items make it easier for you, then go for it. The guest list is sitting at an even dozen, but I want enough for fifteen goodie bags. Just in case."

"Leave it to me," she said.

So I did.

Next on the list was an actual trip to an adult's-only love shop. Since I had to pass a couple of them on my way to work, I showered and got ready, and headed in to work early.

It wasn't until I was behind the bar at Risqué, stocking beer and doing prep work, that thoughts of Harlan refused to be pushed aside any longer.

I liked him. I liked how he made me feel, *what* he made me feel. Talking to him was easy, and there was no question about the sex. The man had a drool-worthy body, and he knew exactly how to use it.

Only after spending the day with him, I couldn't pretend that I was just going with the flow anymore. This was real. He was real.

And I was way out of my element.

Sex I could handle. Meeting for drinks when I had a plan of action, I could handle. But the whole wandering through art galleries and sharing private time with a man who knew my secrets without me even telling them was a whole other game.

We'd barely talked about anything significant, yet, I felt . . . Shit, I didn't know what I felt, but it was *something*.

It didn't matter that Harlan seemed to be the man I'd always wanted, the one I'd been waiting for. My experience with men was sexual only. Working in a nightclub wasn't exactly conducive to dating, what with working when most people were playing. And figuring that when Mr. Right came along he'd see beyond the club clothes and bartender attitude, I'd always liked it that way.

Only now that I had a man who was looking beyond the club clothes and attitude, I wasn't sure how to proceed.

A movement in the top corner of the club caught my eye and I knew Val was stocking the VIP bar upstairs for me.

I loved working for Val, but I loved working for him not only because I get to have a good time at work, but because he was also one of the few people in my life who saw beyond the first layer. He knew that people who stayed in this business too long ended up with issues. Issues with relationships, with drinking, with drugs.

Yet, he'd found Samair. A woman who saw beneath his first layer of tough guy club owner. Proof that it was possible.

Harlan saw beyond my surface. In fact, he saw way too much. He seemed to instinctively know what I needed even better than I did, and as much as I liked it, it was scary as hell.

"Hey, Kelsey. How you doing?"

Callie danced into the bar from the back room, startling me out of my thoughts. I jumped and the knife I was using to slice lemons sliced my finger instead. "Fuck! Fuck, fuck, fuck!" Nothing like lemon juice in a fresh cut to make a person dance and curse.

Sucking my finger I turned to Callie. "Hey, Callie. I'm good. You?"

"Great. Awesome even. I hope it's busy tonight. I need it to be busy. Do you think it'll be busy?"

The waitress's rapid-fire questions told me more than I wanted to know. She was high . . . again. The small-town girl was fast disappearing in the world of easy sex and drugs. "It's Monday. Not a huge amount of people, but plenty of drinking. You know what it's like. You want a drink?"

"Just a diet Pepsi."

I poured the drink and set it on the bar in front of me. "Come and get it."

Callie walked over and grabbed her drink. She avoided my gaze and started to walk away but I grabbed her arm. "Look at me."

Sure enough, her pupils told the truth. "Callie, what are you doing to yourself?"

Her shoulders slumped and she gave me a sullen rebellious look. "What?"

A couple more staff members came in through the back, and after a wave and a smile headed for their stations. When we were alone again I pinned Callie with a stare.

"I'm not your mother, so stop acting like a brat." I sighed and leaned over the bar, trying to get her to see my concern, and not think I was just giving her shit. "I'm asking you what's wrong. Sex in the cooler the other day, and now coming to work fucked up . . . It's not like you, Callie. Talk to me."

She snorted. "Like you're one to talk. You drink all night every night. Everyone here does. George is always stoned and in his own world. Why is it such a big deal that I want to have fun too?"

What could I say that wouldn't be hypocritical? I did drink every night, and a lot of the staff did work high or drunk, it was the way of our world after dark. But Callie had never been like that. She was trying too hard to fit in and it bothered me.

"You're right, drugs and alcohol are common in all night-clubs, and as long as you can do your job, chances are you'll keep it. But Callie, it's not you. What about Rick? How does he feel about you coming home high?"

Tears welled in Callie's eyes. "Rick doesn't care. He dumped me last week."

Crap! I really did not want to get into the whole girly-girl sharing discussion thing with Callie. I wasn't good at it. I could barely handle it when Dee and I did it. But Callie was young, and her whole "love" shtick from before had sort of touched me.

Sigh. "What happened?"

Callie talked and I tried not to tune her out as she went on about how her man had been so busy since they'd moved here. He was in school all day, she worked all night. She was lonely, he was grumpy.

"Y'all seem to have so much fun and my life is so boring."

"It is fun to work in a bar, but it's also a job, Callie." I frowned at her. "You can't be coming to work all messed up or fucking bouncers in the cooler." And if she's so happy screwing around on her boyfriend, why was his dumping her so upsetting?

I shook my head. Who was I to give advice? Relationships confused the hell out of me.

Callie sniffed, then visibly pulled herself together. She

straightened up and smiled. "I'm single and I'm going to have fun now. I want to live life. I want to experience it all and learn by doing, not by reading about it in some book like Rick."

Her words echoed in my ears as I watched her flounce off. She'd sounded just like I did. All that crap about living life and experiencing things—it was the same stuff I'd said to my parents the day I graduated from college. They did not like me traveling the world when I should've been starting a good career. But I'd wanted to live life, to see the world. And I had.

It had been fun. But now there were times when I was more lost than ever before.

Hey, Jack," I said when I looked up and saw my next customer. "How're you doing?"

"Whatever."

I planted my hands on my hips and stared at him. "What's with you?"

"Just give me a beer, Kelsey."

I thought about saying no, just because his attitude sucked and I wasn't in the mood to deal with it, but it seemed a lot of people were having a bad night. I grabbed a bottle from the cooler, twisted the cap off, and slid it over to him. "It's on me, have a good night."

He scowled, tossed a ten-dollar bill on the bar, and walked away with his beer.

"Must be a full moon," I muttered.

Chad, one of the bouncers, was standing at the end of the bar and heard me. He smiled. "You got that right. I caught a couple going at it in the men's john, and Steve's had to ban two people already. He's not in a good mood."

Never mind the big fight we'd all seen earlier when the bouncers between two rival clubs had decided to see who was toughest. Turned out *our* bouncers were the toughest.

It was one of those nights.

Keeping that in mind, I didn't do any drinking, and I didn't push any shooters. Callie bounced up to the bar with an order. I made her drinks, keeping an eye on her as she blatantly hit on Chad.

Chad looked over her head at me and raised his eyebrows.

"Callie," I said. "Stop fucking around and run your drinks out."

"Thanks," Chad said after she'd tottered away with her tray.

Just then, Val walked up. "Send her up to my office as soon as she gets back from that round, Kelsey."

We all watched as Callie stumbled and one of the customers, Jack, caught her with a laugh. Instead of hearing what I'd said about it being a job, she'd gotten it in her head to have more *fun*.

"Her boyfriend just dumped her, Val. She's having a rough night."

He met my gaze. "You gave her a warning last week, and I saw you talking to her at the start of her shift. It's my turn to talk to her now."

Resigned, I nodded.

Val let us drink on shift, but he didn't tolerate drunk and disorderly workers. Risqué was a top club, and the only way to stay that way was to maintain a high level of professionalism while we encouraged everyone else to party hard. I knew he was right about Callie, I'd seen it coming, but losing your boyfriend and then your job was a real shitty week . . . for anyone.

The DJ announced last call and Callie came back from her round. I took her tray and set it behind the bar as the last of my customers walked away.

"Val wants to see you in his office," I told her.

Callie's eyes widened and she bit her lip. "About what?"

"Go see him and find out." I'd already warned her about her behavior before her shift, I wasn't going to get into it with her again.

I watched her walk toward the stairs, passing Jack on his way to the bar. "Beer please," he said.

I twisted off the cap and handed him his order without saying anything. I was tired of babysitting for the night. If he was in a bad mood, I was going to let him stay there.

He took his drink and leaned on the bar. There were no customers behind him and I got the immediate feeling that he'd waited until the last minute on purpose.

"What's up?" I finally asked.

"You fucked Dave."

Oh, *that*.

"Yes, I did." I continued to wipe the bar down, not ignoring him, but not willing to make him my top priority either.

"Why him and not me? I've been trying to get you to go out with me forever."

I stopped my cleaning and looked at him. His frown was fierce and his bottom lip was actually sticking out in a pout! "Jack, I like you, but get real. We both know you've never asked me out."

"I ask you every week!"

"No," I said. "You ask me to go home with you after work every week. That's not the same as asking me out."

"Whatever." His pouting lip disappeared and his posture turned belligerent. "Dave didn't ask you out, and you took him home."

I sighed. Chad and Steve were standing five feet away, watching and waiting to see if I needed them, and I was starting to think I might. "Jack, I took Dave home because he was here when I wanted a fuck and I'd never see him again. You're in here every week, and I'm not interested in dealing with that."

"What's to deal with? We'd have a good time and that would be it."

I threw up my hands. "*This* is what I didn't want to deal with. You thinking you had any say in anything, or anyone, I do. You're a customer, Jack. That's it."

"And you're a fucking bitch!" he snarled. "Thinking you're hot shit when you're nothing but a cunt on—"

Steve snatched Jack's arm, jerked it behind him like a chicken wing, and pushed the struggling guy toward the back door, where Chad stood, backing him up.

I shook my head and poured myself a shot. Definitely a full moon.

Driving home at three thirty in the morning was always nice. Traffic was minimal, and the darkness was comforting, except my mind wouldn't stop racing. Not even Bob Seger on the stereo could distract me from my thoughts.

Callie didn't get fired, but Val suspended her for a week, and told her to get her shit together. Her tears had the other staff hugging her and telling her she'd be all right, and she'd left with two other waitresses—one who'd been working and the other who'd been in the club partying because it was her night off. And as soon as they'd walked out the back door, the others all started gossiping and laughing about it.

Sometimes it really got to me, the way these people all partied together, and shared their secrets and their lives, only to be laughed at or made fun of when they were hurting. Many times I'd compared working in a bar to being in high school again, with all the cliques and the drama and everyone hooking up with everyone else. But it was worse than high school because these were adults. Young adults to be sure, but adults just the same. And the superficial shit just got to me.

Then again, maybe that was why no matter how much I enjoyed my actual job, I didn't feel like I quite fit in at Risqué anymore.

30

My first instinct was to avoid Harlan. It would've been easy too, considering he didn't call me on Monday night when I got home from work. But hiding wasn't my way.

Part of me wanted to just move on, we'd had fun, it was nice, it was over. Roll with it. But the other part wouldn't let it go. I tossed and turned in bed, trying to sleep, but my mind wouldn't shut off.

I couldn't forget the way he slept with me that first night, but didn't fuck me, or the truth in his voice when he'd said he wanted to get to know me, not just take me to bed. The question that kept running through my mind changed from did I want to see him again to . . . did I really believe he could be the one I'd always dreamt of?

He'd watched me fuck myself. He'd watched me get fucked, by more than one guy. He'd watched me jerk off a stranger in a bar . . . and yet he spoke to me with respect—almost reverence.

It was an amazing thing to me. I was used to being judged. Judged by strangers because of my appearance of colored hair, body piercings, and skimpy clothes. Judged by my family because I preferred to work as a bartender instead of something *better*.

I knew there was more to me than met the eye, but it was unusual for a guy to know that.

Overthinking things sucked. I finally flopped onto my back and concentrated on my breathing. Breathe in through the nose, out through the mouth. Good energy in, bad energy out . . . and I drifted off to sleep.

When I woke up on Tuesday morning Harlan was the first thing that popped into my mind. I rolled out of bed and started to dress, and when I pulled out the first T-shirt I'd painted on, I knew it was just the kick in the pants I needed.

A big black men's T-shirt that I'd painted a bright King Protea flower on. The blend of orange and yellow with tinges of pink blended smoothly on the almost prickly looking petals. Fire colors. The flower stood for *daring* and I'd always thought of it as my own personal symbol.

Wearing the shirt, and a pair of cotton shorts I traipsed to the bathroom and did a quick cleanup before heading out the door. I was going to be daring. I was going to spill my guts, and see where Harlan truly stood.

Calling him probably would've been smarter than going over and knocking on his door, but that didn't stop my feet from moving forward.

He answered the door in loose jeans and a thin paint-spattered T-shirt that hung off his broad shoulders. Dark stubble shadowed his jaw, his hair was mussed, and he was barefoot.

How weird is it that I found him being barefoot sexy?

"Hey, stud," I said as I shoved my hands in my pockets to keep from reaching out and touching. "How you doing?"

The distracted expression left his face the instant he saw me. His eyes lit up and his warm voice made my already hard nipples throb. "Great. How are you doing, Kelsey?"

He stepped back and waved me into the loft. I passed in front of him and the light musk of working male tickled my nose, making my sex flutter.

Ignoring the little jolts of sensation that zipped from nipple to groin, I tried to focus on the conversation. "Doing good as well. I just thought I'd come by and say thank you for taking me shopping on Sunday."

"You're welcome."

Hmm, he was not going to make this easy. Why didn't he say anything? Then again, what did I want him to say?

Fuck.

"Thanks for everything else too. The park, and the very nicely done playtime . . . I enjoyed it all."

"I did too." His lips twitched. "I'm glad you dropped by, I was hoping it wasn't too much for you. I didn't want to scare you off."

"Too much?" I snorted. "Hardly. In fact, I was wondering when we could do it again."

Harlan laughed and I cursed silently. That was so *not* what

I'd been planning on saying, but seeing him all rumpled and yummy looking, hearing his voice, and the playful challenge, the words had just popped out.

We stood there for a minute, neither of us speaking until I couldn't handle it anymore. "I'm sorry for just showing up at your door. I should've called first."

The intense emotion in his gaze turned my heart into a trip-hammer and I looked away.

He stepped closer and tucked a loose lock of hair behind my ear. "Don't hide from me, Kelsey."

A tight ball of nerves knotted in my gut and I bit my lip. This was a lot harder than I'd expected. Looking at him, talking to him about more, about the future. It was intense, and more exciting than any flirtation I'd ever had. And a big part of me wanted to ignore it all and pretend it had been nothing more than some naked wrestling. But backing down when I was being called out was not my way, so I met his gaze. "I'm not hiding. I'm right here."

"You are here," he told me. "But you're still hiding too. Don't pretend there isn't a connection between us. Don't lie to me."

"Then don't push me," I snapped without thinking.

I stilled, waiting for his reaction. When he remained silent I chanced a look at him. He hadn't pulled away, but he wasn't pulling me any closer either. Shit.

Fuck.

Ugh!

"Look," I said, placing my hand on his chest, my fingers mindlessly stroking a flat male nipple through his shirt. "I'm not sure what's going on here, but I agree there is something. Can't we just go with it for a while, without trying to attach rules and labels to it?"

His lips curved and he reached for me. "What about 'the hottest sex I've ever had'? Can I attach that label?"

Relief flowed through me. "That's a label I can live with."

He kissed me deeply, then pulled back and looked me over while I fought to catch my breath. "Come on over here. I have some things I've been wanting to show you."

My pulse jumped when I realized he was leading me to his work corner. There were three easels in front of a small table that was pushed against the wall. The table was full of oils, brushes, and cans and the scent of paint and turpentine grew stronger the closer we got to the corner.

Neither of us spoke, Harlan just led me to one of the easels and let me see the canvas set on it.

Shock hit me first, and before it wore off, pleasure followed. It was unfinished, half of it coming to life in every minute detail while the other half was more simplistic . . . but it was clearly a painting of me.

Nude, and stretched across the simple blue white background of the canvas. My head was tossed back, ecstasy clear in the shape of my lips and in every line of my body. My body with my arms pulled behind my back and bound in rope that was wrapped around my chest above and below my breasts, compressing them and making them jut out.

Following the path of the rope with my eyes I saw that it went from the knot between my breasts down the center of my torso and then disappeared between my thighs. The angle of the body showed that the rope was kept taut by being wrapped around my own wrists. It was an incredibly erotic version of being hog-tied.

My voice was husky with arousal when I asked, "What happens if I move?"

"The rope would rub against the folds of your sex, but not directly on your piercing, or your clit. It would work you up, but not get you off."

I tore my gaze from the painting and found him watching me intently, his smile slightly evil.

My breath caught and my sex clenched hungrily.

Before I could say anything else he nodded to the second easel and I stepped past the first. This one was also of me.

It had the same sort of hazy blue white background, but a shade darker. In this one I was blindfolded and tied spread-eagle to a bed with a black metal frame. The restraints looked familiar and my mind flashed on the silk scarves Harlan had purchased on Sunday.

I wasn't alone in the second painting. A large and obviously male shadow loomed next to the bed.

"You?" I asked.

"In my mind . . . yes."

I swallowed hard. Emotions and sensations swamped me, but there were too many to isolate. Harlan stepped to the side of the table, and without a word, started to turn over the canvases that leaned against the wall.

Three more paintings of me, all with a variation of the blue white background, in various forms of undress. Straddling the kitchen chair with my back arched, head flung back. Propped against a mound of pillows, legs spread with one hand covering a breast and the other between my thighs, hiding my sex from view. One of my head and shoulders above the covers as I slept peacefully.

Awe. That was what I felt the most. With arousal and pride running close behind. Harlan stood next to me as I gazed at them, his tension palpable.

I got to the end and turned to him. "They're beautiful," I said. "I can't believe you actually painted me."

His shoulders dipped and I realized just how anxious he'd been about my reaction. Stepping up to him, I wrapped my hand around the back of his neck and pulled him down for a kiss. I rubbed my body against him and slid my tongue against his.

He kissed me back until we were both breathing hard and his erection was pressing against my belly. When he lifted his head he stepped back and held me at arm's length with a small smile. "I'm glad you like them. How do you feel about them being on show?"

Lust fuzzed my brain. Huh? "Like to the public?"

He nodded. "And for sale."

"Very cool," I said. "I think that's great."

"Are you sure? Think about it, Kelsey. I don't have any control over who buys them, and while it's unlikely people who see you will recognize you *from* the paintings, people who know *you* will recognize you in them."

I thought about it for another minute, but it didn't bother

me. The paintings were clearly art, and not just gratuitous porn. My parents could see them and I wouldn't mind.

I might blush, but I wouldn't be ashamed or anything. In fact, the thought of so many strangers seeing me on display so erotically was a turn-on.

"No problem," I said, and pushed against the arms holding me away from him. I was tired of talking, of thinking. I just wanted to feel. "Now, let's get naked."

He opened his arms and pulled me to him with a grin.

My tongue slid between his warm lips and danced sinuously against his. Hot blood rushed through me, the burning need to be closer making me squirm against him, hands clutching him tight. His hands gripped my hips and lifted. Without breaking our kiss, he carried me to the sofa where he dropped down into the seat so I straddled his lap. Lips touched, hands caressed, and our bodies instinctively shifted until we fit together. His hardness against my softness.

My insides liquefied, surrounding the hard knot of arousal growing in my belly. Soft and swollen and wet, I ached to be filled.

Reaching between us, I made quick work of his jeans while his hands ripped open my shorts. One large hand skimmed over my rear while the other slid between the slick folds of my sex.

I gasped at the touch, my hips jerking uncontrollably as a mewl of hunger escaped from me. My hand wrapped around Harlan's hard cock and I stroked it. Up, down, the hot throb of it filling my palm the way I wanted it to fill my sex. My thumb scraped over the smooth head, spreading the wetness there while my hips rode his hand.

"Not enough," I said against his open mouth. "More, Harlan, give me more."

He pulled his hands from my shorts and cupped my ass, surging to his feet and carrying me to the bed. He set me on my feet next to the bed and grabbed a condom from his bedside drawer while I got rid of my clothes. As he was about to roll the condom on, I stopped him. Taking it from him, I sheathed him myself with slow, sure movements.

God, he felt so damn good in my hands!

But he'd feel even better buried deep inside me. I grabbed his shoulders and lay back on the bed, pulling him down so he covered my body with his. With no further encouragement he settled into the cradle of my hips and joined us together.

His mouth went to my throat, nipping and licking, biting and kissing as he thrust deep. I closed my eyes, reveling in the way he filled me. Hitching my hips, I wrapped my legs around his waist and moved with him. Soon, his hands tangled in my hair pulling my head back until my eyes opened and our gazes locked, making our connection complete.

"Kelsey," he whispered, his voice hoarse with emotion.

My heart pounded and my chest tightened. There was more than desire, more than lust darkening his deep blue eyes. Even scarier was the way that look made me feel. Everything inside me melted, that look sending me over the edge as pleasure overwhelmed me.

Harlan's lips parted, his groan of satisfaction mingling with my cries and echoing through the loft. His arms trembled next to my head and I reached up to pull him close, taking the weight of his body on me.

"Heavy," he muttered, and tried to roll off.

"Stay." I tightened my hold on him and spoke softly. "I like you on me . . . inside me."

We dozed for a bit, holding each other, then woke to spend the next few hours wallowing in each other's bodies. When I finally dragged my ass out of bed to go home and get ready for work, Harlan was asleep once again.

I think I wore him out.

Slipping my clothes back on, I started for the door only to have my feet take me back to his work area. The paintings were better than good, and it wasn't just pride or whatever because I was the subject that made me think that. The colors were luminous, the details in each image exact. The talent of the artist was clear, and so was the emotion behind the images.

Everything I'd felt in Harlan's arms came rushing back to me. The heat, the emotion, the comfort, and the contentment. Somehow, our afternoon in bed had been more than an afternoon of sex. We'd been making love.

Panic rose, my heart skipped a beat and the urge to run was too strong to resist. I spun on my heel and headed for the door lickety-split, but Harlan's voice stopped me in the middle of the room.

"Kelsey, you okay?" He was out of the bed and moving toward me fast.

Shit. Fuck. Shit.

Deep breath, I told myself. *You're an adult. You want this.*

Harlan could see her suck air in, then let it out slowly, forcibly relaxing herself. Her lips lifted in a smile that didn't reach her eyes. "I'm fine. I've just got to go get ready for work."

"Uh-uh." He blocked her way. This was it—the withdrawal he'd been expecting ever since the night he'd gone over to her place and they'd fucked each other blind—and he was ready for it. "I saw you over there, and I know something's up. I've watched you enough to know when you're spooked, so spit it out. What are you thinking?"

Kelsey looked up at him, the green of her eyes darkening with determination.

"I'm not a nice girl, Harlan. I like to drink. I like to fuck. I like to do what I want, when I want. I've never had a real relationship. Hell, I'm not even sure I'm capable of one."

Oh, yeah, she was running scared. He'd been surprised to see her at his door earlier, but he shouldn't have been. She was strong, independent, and willful enough to always do the unexpected. But he needed to be careful or he'd lose her before he truly had her. "A relationship isn't a bad thing, Kelsey."

"I know that, Harlan," she snapped. "But that doesn't mean I'd be good at one."

Panic flared to life inside him. She was about to walk away, to leave him in the cold, and he couldn't let her do that.

Quick thinking had him giving herself enough rope to hang

herself. After all, she didn't say she didn't *want* a relationship. Just that she wouldn't be good at one. "Why do you say that, Kelsey? What is it you think you can't handle?"

Her eyes snapped fire and her mouth opened. "I can *handle* anything."

He watched her for a moment, stilling his own temper. Her pulse beat fast at the base of her throat, her eyes darted around, and her hands were twitching at her sides. She expected him to fight. She expected him to pressure her despite what he'd said earlier about labels.

She'd let him watch her from a distance because it had been emotionally safe for her, but in that time, he'd come to know her better than either of them could've predicted. His mind knew her, his body knew her, and his heart knew her.

He knew her well enough to know she wasn't ready to accept any of it . . . if he pushed. She was strong-willed, she had to figure things out on her own, and he had to let her.

"Okay, if you can handle anything, then don't run from what we could have. Just take it one day at a time, no pressure, no strings." He reached for her hands and pulled her against his body. "Maybe a few ropes though, or some silk scarves."

He lowered his head and claimed her lips. He hadn't been able to say all he wanted to say with words, but he could do it this way.

Kelsey stiffened, holding herself away from him for just a second before she melted. Her lips parted and she opened, welcoming him. Heat swept through him, his body tightening with need, *again*, as her arms wrapped around him. She dug her fingers into him and pulled him close, almost purring into his mouth. Small hands slid down his back and cupped his ass, pulling him closer to her as fingers dug into his bare skin.

Until that moment he'd forgotten he was still naked. Kelsey's hand traveled over his hip, seeking out his hard-on, and he stepped back, a rumbling groan rolling out of him.

He grabbed her hand before she grabbed him. "You have to go to work, sexy girl."

Her bottom lip thrust out and he fought back a grin. He swatted her on the ass and walked backward, away from her, toward the shower.

"If you come knock on my door when you get home from work, I'll give you a treat," he called out over his shoulder.

"Promises, promises."

He stopped ten feet away from her and turned. His voice deepened and he pinned her with his gaze, making sure she saw the open desire in them. "If you'll remember correctly, I'm very good at keeping my promises."

Color crept up her cheeks at that reminder. "Yes, you are. I'll see you after work then."

She left and he went to the window to watch her cross the street, the spring in her step putting one in his heart. They were in a relationship, even if Kelsey couldn't admit it to herself.

31

The next day I rolled out of bed around noon, with energy to spare. It was weird. After work I'd parked in my normal spot behind my building, and then walked over to Harlan's. He'd answered the door all rumpled and warm from bed, and proceeded to heat me up over and over again. After dozing in his arms for a bit while I recovered, I'd left him still asleep to come home and crawl into my own bed.

I figured after spending all night awake I'd sleep all day, but it wasn't to be. With maybe four hours of sleep I was wide awake and trying to find ways to keep myself busy so I wouldn't stop to think too hard. The apartment was spotless and I was wiping down the last shelf in the fridge when the phone rang. I grabbed it without looking at the caller ID.

"Hello?"

"Hello there, sexy girl. How are you this morning?"

I glanced at the clock and grinned. "It's almost two in the afternoon, Harlan. Are you just waking up? Did I wear you out last night?"

His chuckle echoed over the phone and my insides warmed. I left the kitchen and walked through the living room to the balcony. The sun was shining, and the air was fresh.

"You didn't even come close to wearing me out," he said. "You're the one who passed out after only three orgasms."

"It was four orgasms."

"Are you sure?"

I grinned, proud. "Yes, I'm sure."

The banter was nice. More than nice, it confirmed that the strange connection we had was more than physical.

An idea struck. "What are you doing this afternoon?" I asked.

"I just finished up a meeting with my agent, and I was thinking I might do some more work. What are you doing this afternoon?"

"I'm craving some real food, so I'm going to go grocery shopping."

"Real food?" The dubious note in his voice had me giggling. *Giggling!*

"As opposed to the microwave dinners and fast food I normally feed myself with."

"Ahh. Gotcha."

Before I could second-guess the urge, I opened my mouth and the words spilled out. "Do you want to come over for dinner before I go to work?"

"Just tell me when to show up." His voice was full of warm affection and it chased my morning-after fretfulness away with ease.

I left the apartment ten minutes later and headed to the market. I had no idea what I was going to make, but I loved to play in the kitchen, especially when I had someone besides myself to feed. Something would jump out at me once I was in the store.

Sure enough, when I walked through the produce aisle the fresh fruit called to me and an image of cold salads and dips popped into my head. After all, it was a summer afternoon, and the fact that dips could be just as tasty on skin as on food didn't enter my mind at all. Nope, not even when I was sure to get caramel and chocolate for the fruit.

I was slicing fruit and singing along with Pink when Harlan arrived. He strode into the apartment and didn't hesitate. I'd barely closed the door behind him when he pinned me to the wall and covered my mouth with his.

Tongues danced and bodies rubbed as my knees went weak and juices began to flow. I cupped his firm ass and pulled him tight to me, sighing at the instant heat that flared between us.

Harlan lifted his head, and breathing heavy, he stepped back. "Hello."

"Wow," I said. "I like the way you say hello."

His lips twitched and he shook his head. "You really are a greedy girl, aren't you?"

Heat flared in my chest and crept up my neck, and I ducked my head before I caught myself. When I lifted my chin and looked at Harlan, it was clear by the serious expression on his face that he'd seen my instinctive reaction.

"Do you remember what I said?" he asked.

I searched my mind. "I remember a few things."

"I told you to see me, and to let me see you." He leaned down and kissed me gently. "Don't ever be ashamed of how we make each other feel, or what we might do to, or for, each other."

Then he grabbed my hand and pulled me into the kitchen. "Now feed me," he said with a grin. "I'm hungry."

I spooned up pasta salad with fresh veggies and a light dressing I'd made myself, and grilled chicken breasts. Nothing fancy, but definitely tasty. Harlan sat at the table and watched me, smiling but not saying anything, and surprisingly, the silence was comfortable.

Working as a bartender had me in and out at strange hours. I slept when most people worked, and worked when most people partied. Part of my job was to make sure that when people partied at Risqué, they had a good time. That meant I was always "on" when I was there. I smiled, I flirted, I spun bottles and tossed them in the air as I made their drinks. Most of the time I loved it, but because it could be so energy sucking, I enjoyed my alone time just as much.

I *needed* that alone time to recharge my batteries and be able to perform when at work. It was why I liked to take off and go lie on a beach somewhere every few months. It was why the only time I had visitors in my apartment was when I brought someone home to fuck. And it was why I never let them stay the night. Yet, as I prepared the plates for Harlan and myself, I wasn't the least bit tense or uncomfortable. Warmth eased through my system and settled over my heart.

It felt strangely right to have him in my home.

When I sat down across from him with the food, conversation came easy. I don't even remember what we talked about. Silly stuff that had me smiling and blushing.

After the meal was finished I glanced at the clock and noted I still had two hours before I had to be at work. Perfect.

I pulled a plate of already cut fruit out of the fridge, and put the small bowls of sauce in the microwave for thirty seconds. I wanted them warm, but not hot.

"What are you up to?" Harlan asked when I set the fruit on the table and smiled at him.

"What?" I said innocently. "I made dessert too."

"Uh-huh." He sat back in his chair and folded his arms across his chest. "I know that look in your eye, and I'm pretty sure it's not hunger . . . for food anyway."

I pulled the sauces out of the microwave and set them on the table with a wink. "Which would you prefer on your dessert, sir, chocolate or caramel?"

He didn't even look at the fruit. Harlan stood and immediately dipped a finger into the caramel, then swiped it across the swell of my breasts. "I think I like caramel."

Wrapping his hands around my waist he lifted until I was on

the table, and then stepped between my thighs. Dessert was better than I could've imagined, and I was late for work.

The rest of the week flew by. My afternoons were full of meetings with Lacey and Lena for party preparation, and after work, my nights were full of Harlan. Each night, I'd park in the lot behind my own building, and think about my big bed upstairs . . . and my feet would take me across the street where Harlan was usually warm and sleepy—and naked—in bed.

He was following the no-pressure track he'd mentioned, and I was starting to accept that we made a good couple. It was freaky that we fit together so well, so quickly. Harlan was an adventurous and attentive lover, not once making me feel too horny or too demanding. Even better, he didn't suffocate me, or bitch about the way I was never there when he woke up in the morning.

Strangely enough, some of the best times with him were just lying in his arms, both of us awake, but not really saying much. Being with him was just that easy and comfortable.

"Man, you so need to get laid."

I slammed an empty shot glass down on the bar and thanked the customer who'd bought it for me with a wink and a smile.

"Me?" I said to John, ignoring the heavy sarcasm and acting innocent. "I think you're projecting there, buddy."

It was Friday night and the bar was full of kids partying it up before the new school semester began. Chad was in his regular position at the door to the back, John and I were working the front bar, our conversation part act for the customers, and part truth.

"Are you saying you're getting some?" John leered. "Wanna share the details? Give me something to think about when I'm all alone?"

I smiled at my next customer and took her money, then turned to my coworker. "If you really want something to think about when you're all alone, think about this." I did a quick spin so my short skirt flared up, and bent over quickly, playfully flashing him my purple thong.

"Such a tease." He snapped his wrist and the tip of the bar towel in his hand smacked my butt.

"Ohh, I like that." I bent over farther and looked over my shoulder. "More please."

The customers lined up at the bar responded with a chorus of "wooo whoos" and some rowdy clapping.

"Give it to her," shouted the frat boy leaning against the bar waiting for his drink.

John twirled the towel and I saw the gleam in his eye. He really was going to give it to me! I laughed and jumped out of the way in just the nick of time.

"Too slow," I said to him, then turned to the crowd. "Who wants a drink?"

John and I worked the bar together smoothly, moving together, switching stations, and switching bottles when needed.

Our banter and our moves kept the customers entertained while in line.

Just before last call was announced the phone behind the bar rang and Val told me to join him in his office as soon as I could. Once the customers were served, and the clock struck two, I left John to shut down the back bar and made my way through the lingering crowd to the stairs.

"Close the door," he said when I entered his office.

I did so, and then flopped into the chair in front of his desk. I stretched my legs out in front of me, and flexed my toes within my boots. God, my feet hurt. I wished I could take my boots off right then, but I'd probably never be able to put them back on if I did.

Maybe I could sweet-talk Harlan into giving me a foot massage by regaling him with the story about Randy's little fetish. I'd discovered that Harlan enjoyed a good dirty story or fantasy.

Fighting back a grin I focused on Val. "What's up?"

"You tell me."

"Nothing much." I shrugged. He'd been in the club all night, and I'd seen nothing that needed to be mentioned.

"Samair tells me you're seeing someone." He pulled a bottle of tequila and a couple of shot glasses from his bottom desk drawer and set them on the table. Muscles stiff, I crossed my legs and watched as he poured two shots. He drank one and nudged the other in front of me. "Tell me about him."

The tequila didn't really call to me, but I threw the shot back anyway before meeting his gaze. "What do you want to know?"

"I want to know what you know."

The ritual with the shots was repeated. This time I held the shot glass in my hand and stared at him, my spine tingling.

He stared back.

"You had him checked out, didn't you?"

"Karl did some snooping for me," he said quietly.

I drank the shot and felt the fire of the tequila battling the flames of anger rising within me.

"You've tapered off on your drinking lately and I don't think I've seen you without a grin plastered across your face. Samair told me how you met and I needed to know the guy wasn't a psychopath." Val sat back and let me stew for a few minutes.

He had no right to do what he'd done, and we both knew it. But battling the anger even better than the tequila, was the knowledge that he cared. He cared enough to not only look into Harlan, but to ask me about him. Which was more than anyone else in my life had done.

Aside from Val and Samair, no one had noticed, or cared enough, to ask me how things were going. Sure, Mom always harped on me about finding a good man and a better job, but that was different. Ariel had picked up on it when we got together a while ago, but I hadn't heard from her since the day I'd set her up with Samair for her dress. Mind you, I couldn't really blame *her* for not asking me for an update since not only had I told her straight up I wasn't going to talk, and her wedding was only a week away.

It was then that I realized just how hurt I was that Dee hadn't called to check on me. The last time I'd talked to her had been my semipanicked phone call about masturbating in front of a guy I liked, and she'd never called back to see if anything came of it.

It wasn't a huge thing, but it hurt that my best friend didn't care about what was going on in my life. Val showed me that someone other than my family cared.

"What did you find?"

He fingered the file on his desk. "Nothing special. Ex-ironworker, new artist who's rumored to be the next big thing. No criminal record, not even a parking ticket."

The tension between my shoulders started to ease. "Don't you feel like an idiot now?" I sassed.

He shook his head. "I'll never feel like an idiot for looking out for my friends."

Emotion clogged my throat. He'd called me his friend, not just his employee. Tearing my gaze from his, I glanced around the room, searching for something to focus on.

When I had control of my emotions and I looked back at him, Val's features softened as he smiled. "There's nothing bad in the report, Kelsey, but I still want to meet him."

"I'm going to come in early tomorrow to set up for Ariel's party, if that's okay with you?"

Val's eyes darkened but he let the subject change go and we talked about the next night for a few minutes before I left.

Thoughts filled my head during the drive home from work. Crazy thoughts.

Once again I felt alone. It was stupid, but I couldn't shake thoughts of Dee. Maybe our friendship wasn't as solid as I'd thought. She'd never hurt me, and there was no doubt that if I called her, she would do anything for me. But if I didn't call her again, would she ever reach out to me?

And what about Harlan? Despite my not wanting to put a label on things, it felt like we matched. When we were together we could joke and laugh, and fuck. And we were just as comfortable not talking, but just *being together*.

Maybe I was just seeing what I wanted to see. Maybe I was just so damn tired of being alone that I was conning myself into believing there was more between Harlan and me than there really was.

This time, when I parked my car, my feet didn't carry me across the street, they carried me up the stairs of *my* building to *my* apartment. I needed to be alone. I needed to think, and figure out what the hell I was doing—what I really wanted. Because it was clear that something in my life needed to change.

I walked in the door and before I took my boots off, I cracked the seal on the bottle of Stoli I'd borrowed from Risqué.

Barefoot, I strolled out to the patio and slumped into my chair. Instead of looking up at the stars, I stared across the street at Harlan's loft.

It was dark, and he was probably in bed, naked and warm, and maybe even wondering if I'd be there soon. Logic told me to call him. Hell, logic also said I was overreacting to everything. But I couldn't stop myself.

I was drowning in a sea of unfamiliar emotions, and I didn't want any witnesses.

32

Harlan watched her, sitting in the dark, alone with her bottle, and his chest ached. He wanted to go to her. To help her work out whatever it was that was eating at her, and he could tell something was definitely there. He could practically feel her vibrating emotions from across the street.

But he'd said no pressure.

So instead, he stood at the window and watched. She'd come to him three nights in a row, and it had been unbelievable. The sex was raunchy and real one minute, and loving and surreal the next. They had a connection. It hurt to watch her sit in the dark and not go to her. With the bathroom light behind him, his silhouette was illuminated and she could see him. That was how she'd caught sight of him the first time, and he used that to make sure she saw him watching her now.

She might need her own space, but he needed her to know he wasn't going anywhere.

As an artist, he knew emotions, and he knew angst. He'd watch her battle whatever was going on in her head, and he'd be there when she was done.

33

"Whooo hoooo!"

I turned at the catcall and watched Ariel jump into the cage with Savannah and start shaking her ass to the music.

My little sister was truly enjoying her party, and it warmed my heart.

While setting up that afternoon, Samair and I had decided that a bachelorette party wasn't complete without a lot of dancing and men to flirt with, but the games and "carnival" were meant for Ariel and her friends only. Therefore, the carnival was in the private room, but I'd decorated the rest of the nightclub with a few balloons and streamers so the women would feel free to roam without feeling like they'd left the party.

The carnival theme had been a surprise to Ariel and her friends, and a huge hit. They'd walked into the private room earlier, been handed their goodie bags of erotic chocolates, a piece of lingerie (a set of sparkly pasties, a small thong, or a teeny-tiny nightie made from some shiny stretch material) and a throwaway camera—and their faces had lit up.

"It's so much more than I'd thought possible, Kelsey. I was expecting munchies, shooter specials, and some dancing. This is incredible," Ariel had said, excitement and emotion bubbling over.

The psychic had been set up in a corner with a gauzy canopy that made it look like a tent. A privacy screen separated the tent from the ringtoss game, where the women had to stand behind a line five feet from a slanted board sprouting three different sized rubber cocks. For two dollars the women got three rings to toss, with different prizes to win depending on which cock the rings landed on. Prizes varied from massage oils to sexy man calendars, silver bullet vibrators to Big Ben.

Samair was manning the ringtoss game for me, and the money would go toward offsetting the cost of the prizes.

Those covered the "talent" and "game" aspect of the carnival with the third one, the "ride" being set up in front of the one-way mirror that looked out into the nightclub's dance floor.

It was a pole, with Joey Kent giving pole dancing and sexy, stripper dance lessons to the ladies.

"Everyone can dance," Joey had said to the group. "Don't worry about a thing ladies. I'm going to prove to you that if you just think sexy while you move, you're going to feel sexy, and you're going to *be* sexy!"

The women had loved it, and from where I stood, it looked like everyone was having a night to remember.

"You did a great job."

"Thanks." I turned to smile at Lacey, who'd come to stand beside me and watch the crowd. "It was actually a lot of fun once I got into it. The food's a hit too. It's what brought the whole theme together."

The whole group had "oohed" and "ahhed" over the erotic ice sculpture of an entwined couple laid out over the table. It housed bottles of beer, coolers, wine, and at the end of it, a stash of chocolate-covered bananas.

"The sandwiches aren't really carnival food, but they're better suited to the women than burgers and fries," Lacey said with a small smile.

She'd made a variety of healthy sandwiches to go along with the fruits and chocolates and mini donuts that served as munchies for the group—and in keeping with the theme of the bachelorette party, the sandwiches were cut in the shape of the male physique.

I chuckled. "That's for sure. But did you see the way that blonde bit the head off hers? She's pissed at some guy for sure."

"She definitely has issues."

Don't we all?

I'd woken up feeling like shit that morning, and not because of the bottle of Stoli I'd opened. After my first drink, I'd done nothing more than hold the glass and wallow in my thoughts. I'd felt like shit because I'd seen Harlan's silhouette in his window, and I hadn't had the guts to call him. I'd been having a temper tantrum and a bout of self-pity, and he'd seen me. How attractive was that?

Lacey spoke again, interrupting my thoughts. "Joey's got your mom working the pole in the private room, and your sister is up in a cage shaking her ass. So why are you just standing here?"

"Just taking it all in," I said. "Making sure everyone is having a good time."

"You're very good at this. Right down to getting Samair and me to donate for the goodie bags in exchange for letting us include brochures of our businesses."

I shrugged. "You guys helped me out by being so quick and flexible with things, why shouldn't I try to help you promote your stuff?"

Lacey nodded, a small smile playing at her soft lips. "Now's not really the time for us to talk, but if you're ever interested in a job as a party planner, I'd love for you to come by Ambrosia and see me." She gave me another smile and walked away.

Shock and pleasure washed over me in equal amounts. A job offer! Not that I was looking for a new job; I loved bartending, but it was a great feeling to know that I'd impressed a professional without even trying.

I heard my name being called and I saw Lena waving at me from under the stairs. She was holding hands with a short dark-skinned guy in jeans and a button-up shirt—only the buttons were only done up halfway and he had some seriously ugly bling.

"Having a good time?" I asked when I stood in front of them.

"It's wonderful!" Lena said with a grin. She introduced me to Joe, the guy standing next to her. "The bouncer won't let me bring him into the private party."

I glanced at Chad, who was acting as doorman for the private room, keeping the public out so the party would remain private. He smiled, laughter at the drunken Lena and her pseudolatin lover companion clear in his eyes.

I nodded. "One guest per woman is cool, Chad."

Lena squealed and hugged me before dragging her man into the room by the hand. I followed them into the room and snatched a beer from the ice bed before going to watch Joey teach my mom how to work the pole.

I got there in time to see Mom slide down with her back against the pole, and then slither her way back up. When she stood again everyone around cheered as she threw back her head and laughed.

"Looking hot," I said when she came down off the stage to stand by my side.

She brushed a lock of hair from her forehead and smiled serenely. "Thank you, dear."

We stood side by side for a few moments and the lack of conversation started to feel uncomfortable. I took a deep breath and made a conscious effort to relax my shoulders. That didn't work so I took a long draw from my beer. That helped a bit.

"Your sister is having a good time," Mom said.

From where we were standing we could see Ariel in the cage on the other side of the one-way mirror—dancing and laughing, tossing her hair and gyrating her hips. "I'm glad. I wasn't sure she'd enjoy the club, but I figured the carnival thing would be fun either way."

"You did a great job with the party, Kelsey. I knew you would."

"Yeah, 'cause I know how to party, right?"

Shit! As soon as the words were out of my mouth I gave myself a mental kick in the ass. All I needed was to get into it with my mother right there and then.

But instead of snapping back, my mom turned to me and put her hand on my shoulder. "No. I knew you'd do a good job because I know you care enough about your sister to take care with all the details that make a party a success."

My surprise must've shown on my face because Mom smiled, her eyes a little sad. "I know I'm always after you about working in this place, but it's only because I want the best for you. No matter how much you say you love it, there's always been a sort of unhappiness in you." She cocked her head to the side and studied me. "Something's changed though, hasn't it?"

I swallowed the lump that had suddenly appeared in my throat. How did I answer that? *Had* something changed inside me?

Before I could say anything, Mom leaned in to kiss my cheek. "I've had a good time, dear. But it's late for me, and if I hurry home I'll have a chance to show your father some of my new moves before he falls asleep." She winked and sashayed away, hips swinging.

Right then, a lightbulb went on so bright inside my head it about blinded me. I'd been feeling like shit all day because pride had kept me from calling Harlan. He'd done nothing wrong, and neither had I. Not really. So he saw me sitting out on my deck pouting, he'd seen me do worse. Sure, it made me feel hurt and vulnerable to know that Dee and I were drifting apart—I'd let her get closer to me than anyone in the past. But that was a long time ago. Max's words had hit me that day in my kitchen, but I'd been thinking of Harlan at the time. Thinking that he'd come into my life when I needed him. But the words applied to Dee, and her easing out of my life as I needed her to.

We'd been nothing more than surface friends for a while and it was time for me to let it go. I mean, how close could we be when I was scared to tell her how I'd met the man of my dreams? And it was time to admit it; Harlan was the man of my dreams.

Was I really going to let a little embarrassment or pride get in the way of that?

No fucking way.

I dashed up to Val's office and found the door closed. After using my own key to get in I sat behind his desk and dialed Harlan's number from memory.

"Hey stud," I said when he answered on the third ring. "What are you doing tonight?"

"Just relaxing with a movie. How's the party?"

Harlan's reply had been smooth and casual, his voice warm . . . and I knew then that I was totally falling in love. The guy could've mentioned my lack of attendance at his place, or my stint on the deck and asked me what was up . . . but he didn't.

"The party is good, only one thing missing to make it great."

"Really? I'm surprised, your plans sounded pretty perfect when you told me about them. What did you forget?"

"I forgot to invite you."

Harlan stood against the rail and watched from above as Kelsey moved among the writhing bodies on the dance floor. She'd sounded great when she'd called, and she looked even better as she did a sensual bump and grind against her dance partner.

She was dancing with a big black guy. Solid muscles and smooth moves described him to a T. Her pale hand rested against the back of his neck, their foreheads touched, and their bodies moved together as if they were naked. Harlan's blood heated and his pulse sped up. Christ, they looked hot!

He wondered if the guy would be interested in posing with Kelsey, for him. In that moment he realized he loved to watch her almost as much as he loved to touch her.

"You must be Harlan."

Tearing his gaze away from the dancing Kelsey, Harlan gave the man standing next to him the once-over. Tall and solid with dark hair and skin, the guy looked like someone who knew how to take care of himself.

"Yes, I am," he answered. "And you must be Val."

There was no reaction in the other man's dark eyes and Harlan bit back a smile. This guy was definitely a guard dog. *Might as well get this over with,* he thought as his pulse jumped and his own instincts came to the fore.

"I'm in love with Kelsey, and I'd never hurt her," Harlan

said, looking Val straight in the eye. "But beyond that, what happens between us is our business, not yours."

Val was silent for a moment, staring at him. Harlan waited. He'd respect the man's protective urges—to a point.

Finally, Val nodded and held out his hand. "As long as you don't hurt her, we'll get along fine."

Harlan shook his hand and they turned as one to look at the crowd below them. There was still a bit of tension there, and it would probably be there for a while. But he wouldn't let it bother him.

He watched as Kelsey spun in her partner's arms. With her back against his chest, she slithered down his body, rubbing and bumping her ass back against his groin as she stood again. Harlan's chest tightened and his cock hardened.

Whatever had been bothering her the night before was gone for now, and he was glad. It had been the hardest thing to not go to her when she'd been out on her deck, but he knew she was strong. And he knew she'd not have welcomed his interference in what she still thought of as her own problems.

It would take time for her to completely trust him, and that was okay. He had all the time in the word when it came to waiting for her.

As if she sensed his eyes on her, Kelsey turned her head and looked directly up at him. Her eyes brightened and she ground her hips against her dance partner deliberately.

Harlan smiled, enjoying the tease. She grinned up at him, then kissed her partner's cheek before leaving the dance floor and making her way to him.

"You seem to be good for her," Val said as they watched Kelsey make her way up the stairs. "Keep it that way."

Val stepped around Harlan and intercepted Kelsey with a few words before continuing on without looking at Harlan again.

"You made it," Kelsey said when she stopped in front of him. "You going to come down and join the party, or hang out up here and *watch* all night?"

"I'm not really in the mood for watching tonight. I think I'll join in."

Their eyes met and Harlan tilted his head, his next words slipping out. "You okay?"

Kelsey's eyes softened and her cheeks flushed a bit. "Yeah, I was just having some issues last night."

"We all have issues."

"True," she said with a small smile. "So what are yours?"

He fought a grin. She was damn quick. "Nothing too bad. Right now I'd say my main one is that I'm falling in love with the most amazing woman, and I'm having a hard time keeping my hands off her."

"Kelsey, baby!" A good-looking blond guy grabbed her from behind in a hug and spun her around to plant a kiss on her lips.

R andy!" I smacked him in the chest and stepped back hastily.

"What? I haven't seen you in a while and here you are, out from behind the bar. How could I resist?"

Shit. I glanced at Harlan, my heart pounding, and panic rising. The timing couldn't have been any worse. My dream man just admitted he was falling in love with me, and not only had he just watched me dirty dance with one guy, but then a man he'd watched me play slightly kinky sex games with literally grabs me away!

"You're supposed to control yourself and act like a man in a bar, not a grabby schoolkid with a squeeze toy," I said before disentangling myself from his arms and stepping back beside Harlan. "Now go play with someone else for a while and I'll talk to you in a bit."

Randy looked at Harlan, then at me, a slow grin spreading across his handsome face. He leaned forward to kiss my cheek and spoke softly. "Yes, mistress."

I watched Randy walk away, dread knotting in my belly. Did Harlan recognize Randy from that day in my apartment?

"Kelsey—"

I turned to Harlan and talked fast, interrupting him before he could take back any of what he'd already said. "He's just a casual lover, Harlan. I was getting tired of one-night stands, and of being alone. He's a nice guy with a bit of a kink streak. He's not anyone important and I'm not going to see him again." I looked up at Harlan and managed to keep my hands off him only by clasping them together and holding tight. "I've always dreamt of finding a man like you. A guy who sees beyond the flirting and . . . and well, the fact that I love sex and—"

"Hush, Kelsey," Harlan said, putting his hands on my

shoulders and giving me a small shake. "It's okay. I know you had a life before me, and I don't expect you to change. I don't mind if you fuck someone else, especially if I can watch." He leaned close and stared deep into my eyes. "But I do mind if you *love* someone else."

My heart stopped, then swelled and kick-started again, thumping against my ribs with a fervor that couldn't be denied. Here was a man who knew me. Who knew my secrets, without me even telling him. Yet, he looked at me with desire and admiration. The emotion in his eyes fed the beast inside me and filled the hole I thought could never be filled.

It wasn't a darkness inside me, it was an emptiness. The drinking and sex had filled the hole, but the effects never lasted because the feel-good high always evaporated. It wasn't real. But Harlan was real. What he offered me was real.

"Only you," I promised as I wrapped my arms around his neck and held on tight.

Dear Reader:

"Losing It" is a short story I wrote a couple of years ago that was previously published by Amber Quill Press. I had great fun with Lacey and Matt and they continue to lurk in the back of my mind. When I was writing *Trouble* and an event in the story needed catering, Lacey and her catering company Ambrosia came to mind. This happened once again in *My Prerogative*, and I thought you all might enjoy getting to see a bit more of Lacey Morgan, so I've included the short story here for your reading pleasure.

Enjoy,
Sasha White

LOSING IT

SASHA WHITE

Lacey Morgan hefted the box of linens higher on her hip and sucked in a deep breath before pressing a manicured fingertip to the doorbell. This was it, her first catering job on her own. Only it wasn't just catering the food; she was getting paid extra to plan the whole party. Lord, she hoped she didn't bite off more than she could chew.

The heavy oak door swung open. Lacey's tension kicked up a notch when Matt McAllister's grinning face appeared before her. He looked even better in person than he did in the photos on his sister Rebecca's walls. How was she supposed to concentrate on business when just being near her friend's brother ramped up her hormones?

"You're early."

Refusing to let him see her nervousness, she smiled back and shrugged nonchalantly. "I wanted to have everything set up. I'll have only one assistant tonight to make sure the entertainment goes smoothly, so that means getting more done before everyone gets here."

He stepped back and opened the door wider. "Come on in." With his blue eyes twinkling naughtily at her, he pumped her for information. "And what is the entertainment tonight?"

She shook her head before breezing past him in search of the kitchen. "We made a deal. I don't have to tell you what I have planned, and you don't have to pay me until the night's over, and then, only if you're completely happy with the party."

"Your assistant isn't a stripper, though, right?" He followed her down the hallway.

Lacey suppressed a sly chuckle. "Nope, not a stripper."

When Matt had called her office, he explained that he'd promised the soon-to-be-groom's fiancée that there would be no strippers or dancers of any kind at the bachelor party. He made it clear he wanted to keep that promise. But despite his pledge, Matt also wanted to host a sexy, unforgettable party. Lacey hadn't had a clue what she would do. She'd just seen an opportunity to get him as a client for her fledgling catering company, Ambrosia, and had jumped in with both feet.

Lacey was sure the only reason he'd hired her for the job was because his little sister was her friend, and Rebecca knew that Lacey wanted Ambrosia to gain a reputation for unique and fantastic catering services. Plus, Rebecca'd probably bullied him a bit.

But that was okay; Lacey would take his business any way she could get it. And she felt confident Matt would be very pleased with what she had arranged.

With that thought in mind, she located the kitchen and set the box on the counter. Turning to face him, she laughed at the playful mock puppy dog expression on his handsome face. "Please?"

She ignored the twinge of excitement in the pit of her belly, and gave him a practiced, thoughtful look. "I'll bet not many people can resist when you look at them like that and say 'please' really pretty, can they?"

"Can you?"

"I can," she said firmly. "And I will."

The dubious expression on his face gave her a small thrill. He was so cocky that a new idea sparked in the back of her mind.

"Just because you're the host doesn't mean you can't enjoy the party too." She gave him an obvious once-over and a wink before brushing past him on her way back to her catering van.

She had never planned a bachelor party, but she'd been trying to get her catering company off the ground for a couple of months and figured this might prove to be the edge she needed to make her business stand out from the others. The fact that she had to plan a sexy and classy party with no strippers, or even a belly dancer, also motivated her more than stumped her. She'd also been too intrigued.

Hell, she'd been intrigued by everything about Matt from the moment she'd walked into Rebecca's apartment three years earlier and seen his pictures. But friends didn't ask to be set up with their friend's brothers, so she'd left well enough alone. The party idea, however, had opened that long-closed door.

Now, Lacey couldn't help but feel the seductive pull of lust tugging at her insides as she made several trips from the van to the kitchen, bantering with him the whole time. She was a bit surprised at how comfortable she felt around him, even with her head full of business anxiety and half-baked seduction plans.

He was one sexy man, but he knew it. He also knew just how to flirt with his eyes, and how to use his deep voice so that shivers danced down Lacey's spine. Images of slow, sensuous lovemaking filled her head, but the fact that his confidence bordered on arrogance had her battling the urge to try and master him.

This is business, she told herself. Pleasure would come afterward . . . if he could handle it.

When the van was empty, Matt offered to park it at the side of the house. She gladly handed over her keys, and then wandered back to the kitchen, forcing herself to focus on the task at hand.

The house's setup was a good one, perfect for what she had in mind. She was standing in the patio doorway, gazing at the fenced-in yard, when Matt strolled into the kitchen.

Without looking, she knew he had positioned himself directly behind her. It was as if a force field of energy surrounded him, and when he stood inches away from her, her body hummed with carnal recognition. "Dinner can be served inside or out. Which would you prefer?"

"Whatever works best for what you have planned," he said, his voice deeper than before.

His hands settled on her shoulders and he shifted closer behind her. Lacey closed her eyes. She enjoyed the heat of his touch, and the knowledge that he was coming on to her, very subtly. Him pressing lightly against her backside, his breath tickling the tiny hairs on the back of her neck, were both seduction techniques. Practiced seduction techniques, ones she, herself, had used before.

"Is it usually so easy for you to seduce women?"

He stiffened for a brief moment, then a relaxed chuckle tumbled from his lips. "Honestly? Yes, it is."

Lacey turned from the yard and gave him a small smile. "Then I guess it's time for a change, yes?"

The skeptical rise of his eyebrows gave her another thrill. Seducing him was going to be so much fun.

"I think outside will be best." She continued into the middle of the kitchen and started to unpack her things. All business, as if she didn't feel the spark of lust flaring to life inside her. It wouldn't do for him to know just yet how much she wanted him. "You said you would stock the bar. Is it ready to go?"

His eyes narrowed, and he planted his hands on his lean hips. "Both the inside and outside bars are well stocked with my friends' preferred whiskey."

"Good. Then your work for the night is through. As I said before, you're the host, but that doesn't mean you can't enjoy the party." She picked up the carryall that held the gambling paraphernalia she'd need later that night. After giving him a sassy wink, she walked onto the patio, speaking over her shoulder, "And I plan to make tonight a very memorable night for everyone."

A memorable night, huh?

Matt realized he was actually licking his lips while watching Lacey's rounded hips swing gently as she left the kitchen. Not many women walked away from him, but he sure did enjoy the view of this woman doing it.

Heat pooled in his groin. His hands tingled as he imagined gripping those hips and—

Whoa! This was one of his sister's best friends! Flirting was one thing, but Rebecca would never forgive him if he broke Lacey's heart. And since he had no intentions of getting serious with anyone, that meant Lacey's ass had a big neon Hands Off sign attached to it.

Swallowing a sigh, he blocked the patio door as she started to reenter the house, the empty storage carrier in her hand.

"Let me get that for you." He wrapped his arms around the container, but couldn't stop himself from brushing his hands across her flat stomach while gripping the edges of the armload. Her body heat radiated through her shirt and seeped into his skin. His blood heated and his cock started to swell. The spicy yet soft scent that filled his nostrils when he leaned close certainly didn't help matters either. Clutching the armload to his chest, he turned and crossed to the other side of the counter, giving himself shit as he went.

Keeping his mind and his hands off her would be a bit more difficult than he'd thought. After setting his load on the counter, he strove to look casually at her. "Can I help you set anything up?"

"You don't mind taking direction from a woman?" She quirked an eyebrow at him, her green eyes shining with playful challenge, and her lips tilted up at one corner. Was she mocking him?

"Not at all. Why would I?"

She started unpacking linens from another container. "I just wondered if you—being such a big sports guy, macho man and all—had a problem with it." Humor colored her voice. "Some men seem to think it's unmanly to take orders from a woman."

"Not all men. When it comes to stuff like food and party settings, I'm more than willing to take direction from a woman."

Her tongue darted out and slid across her lips, leaving them glossy and wet. She had the kind of mouth that gave a man an instant hard-on. "Oh? So when it comes to 'women's work' you're okay with taking direction, but that's it?"

Something in her voice reached through his lustful thoughts and made him lift his gaze to her eyes.

Uh-oh. She had that look, the look a woman gets when she's got something up her sleeve.

"Umm . . . umm . . ."

My God, she has me stuttering! Enough was enough.

He drew a deep breath, then flashed his megawatt sales-pitch smile, holding up his hands in a mock defensive gesture. "I didn't say that. I know better than to call anything 'women's work' or 'men's work.' I'm an equal opportunity kind of guy."

The glint in her eye noticeably brightened. "So . . . if a woman were to tell you what to do in the bedroom, you'd be okay with it?"

"Hell, no!" he exclaimed, but his dick jumped behind his zipper, despite his protest. "I don't need anyone to tell me what to do in the bedroom. I've been pleasing women since I was fourteen."

"What if letting her direct you gave her pleasure? Would you let her do it?"

"Matt!" a man's voice called. "Where are you?"

"In the kitchen," he yelled back, disappointed at the interruption. He leaned close to Lacey, deliberately invading her personal space, and spoke in a low voice. "We'll finish this conversation later?"

Not giving so much as an inch, she grinned at him. "You bet we will."

H it me."

Lacey gazed into Matt's vibrant blue eyes and squeezed her thighs together. Oh, how she wanted to bend him over the picnic table and do just that. Spank his nice, firm ass until the cheeks glowed rosy red and he begged her to let him please her.

Instead, she raised an eyebrow and smiled wickedly at the four other men gathered around the stand-up bar. "What do you think, boys? Is Matt making a mistake? Didn't I tell you all to trust me?"

Three of the men hooted and hollered and agreed with her. Only Craig, the groom's brother and the youngest of the group, slapped Matt on the back and encouraged him to go for it.

When the guys had arrived, Matt had led them into the yard, where they made themselves comfortable on the deck chairs and started drinking. When Lacey went out to meet them, they'd stood up and introduced themselves in such a gentlemanly way that she worried for a few minutes her plans would bomb. Hoping to break the ice, she looked at the untouched platter she'd set in the middle of the table.

"What's wrong, guys? No one likes mushroom, truffle oil, and cheese fondue?" The men looked at the food with such blank expressions, that Lacey couldn't help but laugh. "Or is it the fact that the dippers are asparagus, zucchini, and cherry tomatoes? What? Did you expect me to serve chips and peanuts? Don't be scared of it, gentlemen. It won't hurt you." With a small smile, she gave them a hint about the night to come. "In fact, it'll probably make you feel better than you have in a long time."

They smiled uncertainly, probably thinking she meant it in an "eat your vegetables" way. She cocked an eyebrow at Matt, who quickly took the bull by the horns and reached for a zucchini stick and dipped it. With no hesitation, he slipped the morsel into his mouth and started to chew.

Lacey tried not to show how the movement of his strong jaw and the look of pleasure that shone in his eyes affected her insides.

"It's amazing, Lacey. Thank you." He reached for another one.

The others followed suit. While they chewed, nodding and nudging one another over the good taste, Lacey planted her hands on her hips and eyed them in a stern fashion.

"Now, when I say trust me, you are all going to do so, right?"

A chorus of affirmative moans and heads bobbing yes set the tone for the night. Satisfied, Lacey had returned to the kitchen, leaving the men to eat and joke around. When she returned a short time later with another plate, this one full of salmon rounds with white wine and capers, they didn't hesitate.

She'd wondered if they would have hesitated if she'd told them the appetizers were considered aphrodisiacs.

Now, watching Matt, with his wicked grin and the daring glint in his eye, she doubted it would have slowed him down.

He winked at her, tossed back the last ounce of whiskey in his glass, and tapped a long finger on the cards in front of him. "This fourteen isn't enough to beat your eighteen. We're playing Las Vegas Strip, with two decks, and there're enough face cards showing that I think I'm safe."

"Care to make a personal bet on that?" she countered.

The men "oohed" and started whispering amongst themselves, betting on Matt or Lacey, but not interfering in their byplay.

"What do you have in mind?" he asked.

"You break, you owe me . . . a favor of my choice."

"And if I don't break?"

"If you don't break, I'll owe you."

Fire raced through Lacey's veins. The thrill of the risk. She didn't know for certain if he would break. Nothing was guaran-

teed, that's why it was called "gambling," but she'd been playing blackjack since she'd learned how to count, and she knew
the odds were on her side.

"Deal."

Her subtle flirting hadn't gone unnoticed by the rest of the
men, and sexual tension thickened the air. The others sighed or
asked why they hadn't received the same bet when they'd made
a dumb move. But Lacey ignored them and locked eyes with
Matt. With a slow flick of her wrist, she pulled the next card
and turned it over. Neither of them broke their stare to look at
it, until the group's laughter and jostling nudged Matt so hard
he almost fell off his stool.

The Jack of Spades. Busted.

Matt tossed his hands in the air and gave her a cocky grin.
"I'm all yours, sugar. Whatever you want, I owe you."

Warmth flooded through Lacey and her panties dampened
at the obvious lust in his heated gaze. She knew exactly what
she wanted, and from the sparks arcing through the air between
them, she felt certain he would enjoy giving it to her. But before
they got to what she really wanted, he needed to be taken down
a peg or two.

She gave him a small smile. "You're going to help me clean
up tonight, Matt. My assistant will appreciate getting off work
early."

His grin froze, and his buddies laughed even louder. She
knew they'd all been expecting something much more flirtatious as a favor . . . and that was exactly why she wasn't going
to give it to them.

"Okay, boys, card game's over." Lacey pulled her gaze away from Matt and spoke in her firm voice. "Go into the house and pour yourselves another drink while I set up the food."

She watched as the five men headed inside, stumbling just a little as they laughed and playfully shoved at one another. They were like a bunch of rambunctious puppies, except sexier.

Lacey restrained herself from commanding them all to strip and kneel at her feet . . . just barely. Oh what fun she could have with the group of them.

What fun she *was* going to have with them.

Matt was the last one to enter the house, pausing to flash her a wicked grin over his shoulder.

Lord, but that man was hot! Treating him like all of the others had been extremely difficult, but she knew it wasn't time to let him see her interest. Normally she didn't like to play head games with men, at least not outside of the bedroom, but Matt was special.

At first, she'd just wanted him as a conquest, but over the past few hours that idea disappeared. She found herself actually wanting him. Not just the conquest of one of Vancouver's top bachelors, but Matt himself.

She gathered up the cards and empty glasses left on the bar, then went to the kitchen to see how Beth was doing with the food preparation.

"Are you just about ready?"

The tiny brunette looked up from the tray of sushi she'd just pulled from the catering cooler. "I think so." An eager grin spread across her delicate face. "Are they?"

An answering smile tugged at Lacey's lips. "I don't think they have a clue. But as soon as we get you set up, they might be more ready than you want them to be. You remember the safe word?"

Beth's whole demeanor changed. Her spine straightened and she clasped her hands together behind her back, thrusting her perky breasts forward. Her dark eyes flashed before she cast her gaze toward the floor and spoke softly.

"Yes, mistress, I do." She was eager to please, and to fulfill a fantasy of her own at the same time.

"What is it?" Lacey questioned sharply.

"Sunburn."

"Very good." She smiled at Beth and brushed a tender thumb across her smooth cheek. A minute tremble went through the other woman and Lacey's body tingled all over. She was responsible for what happened to Beth tonight, and that thought was one of the many that kept her on the edge of arousal. "I'll be here, and I'll look after you."

"Yes, mistress."

"The table is set up outside. Lay out the cloth and get yourself ready. I'll follow with the food."

Shot down, Matt!" Brian slapped him on the shoulder and leaned on the oak bar in the recreation room, a shit-eating grin on his face. "I don't think I've ever seen you get turned down by a woman."

"She didn't turn me down," Matt corrected amidst the

laughter. "I haven't made a move yet, therefore she hasn't shot me down yet."

"You keep thinking that, buddy," Cole said, pouring a round of whiskeys for the group. "I have to admit, I wondered what the hell we were going to do to send Brian off in style, but so far, your girl's done a good job."

A surge of pride burst in Matt's chest, not because Lacey was doing a good job, but because Cole had referred to her as Matt's girl. Somehow, during an evening of lusting after her, she'd become more than just a pretty girl to him. The neon Hands Off sign had dimmed because he actually liked her.

"Since she shot down Matt, maybe I'll give it a go." Craig leered at the others. "She's nice looking, and damn sexy. You know what they say about older women and younger men. I could be just what she needs."

Matt's gut churned, and he clamped a tight rein on his temper. Relaxing his clenched jaw, he slapped Craig's shoulder and gave him a warning squeeze. "I told you, she didn't shoot me down. Even if she did, she's way too much woman for a young pup like you to handle."

Loud laughter and more smart-ass comments came as conversation turned away from Lacey to the topic of women in general, and how, at twenty-four, Craig still had a lot to learn about them.

Matt stared into his glass of whiskey and melting ice, the color reminding him of Lacey's eyes when she'd been flirting with him. She had been flirting with him; there was no way all the sexual sparks had come off of him alone. The attraction he'd felt for her had been instant and intense, just like his anger at the thought of Craig, or anyone else, hitting on her.

Man, he had it bad.

He'd help her clean up after the party, no problem. He'd keep his hands to himself and ask her out like a true gentleman when he was done. This was one woman he didn't want getting away.

"Dinner's ready, boys." Lacey's husky voice echoed down the hallway.

The guys, eager to sample more delicious food, picked up their highball glasses. Matt led them to the kitchen.

Lacey was stationed at the door to the patio. The beautiful woman was clearly a sexual creature. The sight of her full lips, and her nipples poking against her starched white shirt, made Matt's cock twitch and his palms itch. Keeping his hands off her tonight was going to be hard. Well, he grimaced mentally, "hard" seemed to be the theme of the night anyway.

Earlier, he'd felt he was getting somewhere when she'd made that bet with him. He swore he saw visions of personal massages and oral sex swimming around in her steady gaze. Then she'd shot him down with cleaning duty. For the first time in as long as he could remember, he didn't know where he stood with a woman. And it only made him want her more.

Lacey had pulled the curtains shut across the sliding glass doors so the men couldn't see what awaited them.

"Follow me, gentlemen." She steadied herself, then led the way outside and to the side of the deck.

She stopped several feet from the picnic table and turned sharply on her heel when someone uttered the first surprised gasp.

"Oh, God," Brian said in awe.

Lacey watched as each man stopped dead and stared at the feast. She tamped down her own raging hormones and forced herself to breathe. This was the critical moment in the night. It would set the tone and tell her if Ambrosia could count these influential men as part of her client list.

Lilting oriental music filled the air, and several lanterns gave the small area at the side of the deck a warm, intimate glow. Centered in the dimly lit area stood the picnic table, its crisp white linen cloth contrasting sharply with the tanned skin of the body stretched out on top of it.

Sushi, sashimi, and tempura-battered veggies and prawns covered Beth's bare flesh. Colored flower petals and leaves strategically littered her breasts and belly, while a small porcelain plate with pickled ginger and wasabi waited in the juncture of her thighs, hiding just enough of her hairless pussy to tease.

Lacey waved a hand at the picnic table. "Well, gentlemen. Sit." A buzz hummed through her as the men began to grin like kids in a candy store. The wonderment on their faces told her she'd already succeeded in making this party memorable. "This is Beth, gentlemen. She's my assistant, and she's happy to be able to make your meal most enjoyable."

As the men circled the table, Lacey tried not to smirk at the guilty pleasure clearly stamped on their faces, the hedonistic feast captivating and arousing them. She relaxed, letting the testosterone-filled air seep into her pores and getting her own inner juices flowing.

Once the men seated themselves around the table, Lacey placed a heated cloth in each of their hands. Without thinking, she caught Matt's eye. He'd been looking at her, not the Nyotai Mori–style dinner. Her breath caught in her throat at the look in his eyes, and she suddenly realized there was much more to gain than a client list. She'd felt the sexual tension between them, but his eyes held more than lust in them. She saw pride, and . . . affection?

Feeling just a little bit shaken, she waved a hand over Beth's still form and stepped back. "Bon appétit."

his is dinner, gentlemen. Not dessert." Lacey's voice was laced with humor, and her eyes twinkled when she met Matt's gaze.

Craig lifted his hand from where his finger traced the curve of Beth's breast and reached for a slice of salmon sashimi. Matt's lips twitched, and he shared a soundless laugh with Lacey. Their silent communication was swift and sure. And something he'd never felt with another.

By the time the food was almost gone, the men's "serving dish" hadn't moved an inch. The only sign that Beth was a real woman was the minute rise and fall of her chest, the way her nipples deepened in color and tightened whenever anyone reached for another bit from that area, and the hint of female arousal that tainted the air.

Yet, it wasn't the sight of the naked woman on the table that made Matt's heart pound and his dick throb. It was the clothed woman who stood five feet away—aloof, yet radiating a tightly leashed aura of power.

Lacey moved forward. "Everyone had enough?"

Brian made a show of chasing the last oyster across Beth's belly. He dug it out from beneath the dip bowl right over Beth's pussy, then lifted it flamboyantly high in the air before dropping it onto his tongue. As he swallowed, he moaned in pleasure and wagged his eyebrows at Lacey. "What's for dessert?"

As the others laughed and looked to Lacey for answers, Matt fought the growl building inside him. Brian wasn't flirting with Lacey. He was getting married in three days. He was no threat.

Besides, it was obvious all the guys were pretty focused on the naked woman in front of them, and the option for dessert.

When Lacey walked toward Brian with a sinful grin on her face and a tray in her hands, Matt clenched his jaw so hard he felt pain. Why was she smiling at Brian like that? She should have eyes only for him.

He closed his eyes at the thought. Jesus! He gave himself a mental head shake. He needed to get a grip, and fast.

"If the rest of the group will step aside for a few moments, Brian, since you're the groom-to-be, you can help me get dessert ready."

The men did as she asked, watching as Lacey set the tray by Beth's feet and unloaded a bowl of steaming water.

She handed Brian a clean white cloth. "I'll collect all the

dishes while you clean up our 'serving tray.'" She started picking up the platters.

Brian just stood there.

"Go on man," Craig urged. "Clean her up."

Steve and Rob chimed in with their encouragement, but Matt took another step backward and tried not to breathe fire when Brian leaned in and whispered something in Lacey's ear.

Lacey smiled and assured Brian that touching Beth, and washing her everywhere—even with his tongue if he wanted—was exactly what she'd had in mind. "Beth volunteered for this, Brian. It's a fantasy of hers to be the center of attention for a group of men."

She walked away, hands full of dirty plates and half-full bowls of soy sauce, wishing she could've stayed and helped Brian, but knowing tonight was work, not play.

She set the dirty dishes on the kitchen counter and grabbed the prepped dessert tray from the fridge. When she stepped onto the deck, Matt immediately took the tray from her.

"Where do you want it?"

Before answering, Lacey glanced around. It pleased her to see that the rest of the men had crept closer to where Brian was "cleaning off" Beth, yet no one but him was touching her. It was almost as if they were afraid she'd take away their treat if they misbehaved. Beth was being the perfect centerpiece and hadn't moved, except to spread her legs for him, so Lacey focused her attention on Matt.

"Over there, but not yet." She stepped around him, staying close and lightly trailing her fingertips over his bulging bicep. "First I want to get a better feel for you."

"Feel away," he said, his voice stoking the fire between her thighs.

Lacey scraped a fingernail across the back of his neck and sighed at his slight shiver. She stopped at his side and leaned in closer, her breasts pressing against his arm. She brought her mouth close enough to his ear so her breath would tickle him. "So responsive, Matthew. Do you have a sensitive neck?"

His throat worked as he swallowed. "I seem to have sensitive 'everything' where you're concerned."

Orgasmic moans traveled on the night air, over and above the hushed murmuring of the men by the picnic table.

Matt started to turn.

"Don't look!" Lacey commanded. "Look at me instead."

He met her gaze, and Lacey clearly saw the inner struggle in him. He'd surprised even himself by obeying her, by standing so still while she touched and teased him.

She smiled and cupped his jaw, desperately wanting to kiss him. Instead, she ran her thumb over his bottom lip and took a deep breath. It was time to let him know what she was all about.

"Poor, Matthew. Big, strong, and cocky enough to think he'd never need to take direction from a woman in order to please her. I can see you want me." She ran her other hand up his thigh, cupping the hardness of his erection through his jeans, measuring him, teasing them both. "I can feel how much you want me. But the only way you can have me is to let me teach you how to please me."

It was one of the most difficult things Lacey had ever done, but she stepped back and waited for his reaction. Beth's pleasure cries grew louder, but Lacey refused to look, or stop them, unless she heard the safe word.

Heat arched between Lacey and Matt, him standing rigid, still holding the tray, and her standing directly in front of him, waiting. Neither of them moved, nor spoke, as Beth's cries reached a crescendo and the men cheering her lifted their voices even higher.

A deep trembling started in Lacey's muscles at the fire in Matt's eyes. Unable to wait any longer, she said, "When you're ready," and started toward the picnic table.

With the men surrounding her, a smiling Beth had her eyes closed.

"Is she clean enough to eat off of, Brian?" Lacey asked.

"Oh, yeah, she's clean enough to eat, period."

The men laughed, and Lacey forced out a small chuckle. She really didn't feel like laughing, especially when Matt stepped up beside her and set the tray on the edge of the table.

"Okay, boys, have a seat again."

While the men arranged themselves around the table, Lacey stroked Beth's hair back from her forehead and cupped the sides of her head. Bending forward, she whispered in Beth's ear, "Are you okay?"

Beth's eyelids lifted, and her unfocused gaze met Lacey's. "Oh, yes, mistress. Please continue."

Lacey bent lower and pressed her lips to Beth's soft ones. All five men remained silent, watching the play between the women. The heat of their gazes ignited Lacey's arousal, turning it from a banked fire to a steady flame.

She smiled and picked up the dessert tray. Balancing it on the palm of one hand, she walked around the table and set bowls of peeled and sliced fruit in front of the men. Peaches, grapes, mangoes, figs. A couple of aerosol cans of whipped cream joined them, along with crystal dishes full of chocolate or caramel.

While vigorously shaking an aerosol can, she tilted it and sprayed cream over Beth's perky, hard-nippled breasts. She strolled down the table, her arm held above the men's heads, raining fluffy white cream along Beth's belly, pooling a bit at the juncture of her thighs.

She snagged a slice of mango, dipped it into the whipped cream covering Beth's shaved pussy, and held it to her lips.

"A simple dessert, boys, but one I'm sure you'll enjoy."

The men needed no further encouragement. They reached for food and started playing it all over Beth's body. Craig added some chocolate to the cream over Beth's pussy before dragging a banana through it. He smirked just a little as he nudged the fruit through the cream. The banana bumped against Beth in a way that made her thighs twitch and tremble, her low moan echoing over the group.

Lacey watched as Matt picked up a peach slice and slid it through the sauces smeared across Beth's left breast. To Lacey's surprise, he turned his gaze straight into her eyes before trailing his tongue up the fruit and suckling it before pushing it into his mouth.

Her insides clenched, and now her thighs trembled in response. To hell with making him wait, since she didn't want to wait anymore.

She strolled to the end of the table and stood by Beth's head, stroking the soft hair spread out around the woman's shoulders with her fingers. She smiled into Beth's eyes and slowly reached out a hand. The men froze as Lacey's fingers clamped onto one of Beth's hardened nipples. She lightly squeezed. When Beth arched her back and a pleasured gasp escaped her lips, Lacey winked naughtily at the men.

"It's time for the real dessert gentlemen. I give you one rule, hands and mouths only."

Leaning forward, she replaced her fingers with her tongue and laved Beth's rigid nipple before sucking the nub into her mouth, enjoying the sweetness of the cream and the tartness that was Beth. She backed up and smiled wickedly at the men's shocked faces. "Enjoy," she said, dragging a lone finger across her bottom lip to wipe away any lingering cream.

When she returned to the kitchen, Lacey wanted desperately to look back and see if Matt was following her or playing with Beth and his friends. Instead of looking, she stepped to the side and stood with her back to the wall, eavesdropping. Though she'd gotten a good "feel" for the group and didn't think the guys would get out of control, she still wanted to be within hearing distance in case Beth called out the safe word. After all, it was Lacey's responsibility to make sure nothing happened to the girl.

Plus, her knees were trembling so badly she needed the wall's support. She didn't know why she'd insisted on taunting Matt earlier. Well, other than the fact that touching and teasing him so openly made her knees weak and her pussy drool.

Shit! She'd probably blown it.

He stepped through the open door. When he saw her, he immediately invaded her space, pressing her into the wall with his body.

Hands planted against the wall on either side of her head, he swooped down and covered her lips with his own. His tongue thrust into her mouth, delving deep, tasting her, marking her, and making her moan. She pulled him closer.

His strong fingers wrapped in her hair, and he pulled back slightly, nibbling and suckling at her lips. For a brief moment, Lacey wanted to fight him, to master him, and she pushed against his shoulders, trying to regain control.

A low growl rumbled up from him. He grabbed her hands, pinning them to the wall above her head, and held them in place with one of his. With his other hand, he cupped her jaw and tilted her head to the side, running his teeth down her neck and nipping at her ear.

"You have been driving me crazy all night. And as much as I loved watching you run the show outside, it's not going to happen in here." He bit her bottom lip, then spoke slowly and clearly when she pulled back. "If you want me to stop, just say so, and I'll walk away."

She said nothing.

Matt used his free hand to grope one of her breasts through

her shirt, his fingers scraping across the nipple, then shoved one of his knees between her thighs, making her mind go blank with lust. Her body took over, and she rubbed against his hard leg, her clit swelling, reaching for what friction it could get from her damp panties and his denim-covered muscle.

She lifted a leg and wrapped it around his hip, tugging him closer. She heard Beth's cries of pleasure getting louder, and they fuelled her own arousal. She bit down on his neck, then laved the bite with her tongue. A moan escaped her lips as she uncontrollably rubbed her body against his. "God, yes. Hurry, Matt . . . I can't wait any longer."

Groaning, he released her hands and yanked her skirt up around her waist. Seizing her ass cheeks, he lifted her and used his hips to keep her braced to the wall.

Their foreheads pressed together. Lacey gazed into his eyes and panted, trying to catch her breath while undoing his zipper at the same time. With an impatient grunt, she finally shoved down his jeans past his hips and wrapped her fingers around his cock.

"Ahhh . . ." Their sighs and groans of pleasure mingled as she squeezed and felt him throb in her hand. "Now, Matt," she commanded breathlessly.

He reached between them and shoved aside her thong, dipping a finger inside her wetness. "You're so ready for me," he said, awe coloring his voice as he added another finger.

"Yes . . . you . . . now . . ." Once Matt removed his hand from her, Lacey placed the head of his cock at her entrance and thrust her hips forward, taking him inside.

He sank his body fully into hers. Once again, he held her wrists to the wall, then met her gaze. "I'm willing to take instruction from time to time, but we both know I can please you without it."

He began to move, thrusting in and out, fast and hard. Lacey's back hit the wall, but she didn't care, as long as he kept fucking her. Her insides tightened and the fire in her belly spread outward. Her nipples scraped against his heaving chest, and his hot breath dusted across her skin. With a whimper on her lips, she closed her eyes and every muscle in her body strained toward release.

Matt's mouth came down on hers. He bent his knees, slightly changing the angle of his entry, pushing her over the edge.

When the fireworks inside her body subsided and she came back to herself, she grew aware of his hands gripping her hips and his cock twitching inside her. He fought to catch his own breath.

After a few moments of contented silence, broken only by another round of Beth's orgasmic cries and the mingling cheers and groans from the men outside, Matt pulled back. "If we do this—this relationship thing—is Beth a part of the package?"

She looked at him, wondering if he wanted her to be. "Actually, no. She's a submissive, but not mine. She belongs to a close friend who's into that lifestyle. I've dabbled at being Dominant, but for me, it's an escape, not a lifestyle. They both know this, and since one of Beth's ultimate fantasies was to be the center of attention for a group of strangers that she'd never see again, I asked if she'd be willing to take part in tonight's party." She bit her lip, then unwrapped her legs from around his waist, feeling the need to distance herself a bit. "You'd just be getting me."

"You're all I want." He hugged her tight and placed a soft kiss on her forehead. "And I'm willing to take direction, at times, if you're willing to lose control at others."

She giggled and snuggled against him. "I think it's clear I just lost it." She gazed into the depths of his blue eyes and saw nothing but acceptance, and, surprisingly, love. "How about if we take turns losing it?"